2013:
The End?

Matthew J Krengel

Copyright © 2012 Matthew J Krengel
All rights reserved.
ISBN: 1477533036
ISBN-13: 978-1477533031

DEDICATION

To the many idle hours spent watching the History Channel and all the conspiracy theories surrounding the Mayan Calendar.

CONTENTS

	Acknowledgments	i
1	Category Six	Pg 1
2	Temple of Time	Pg 11
3	The Codex	Pg 19
4	Burning Sky	Pg 25
5	Path To Power	Pg 33
6	Time Passes	Pg 41
7	Like Magic	Pg 47
8	Unexpected Blessings	Pg 53
9	Dec 15, 2085	Pg 63
10	Maria	Pg 73
11	One Kiss	Pg 85
12	Goodbye	Pg 95
13	Return to the Temple	Pg 97
14	The Spirit Realm	Pg 107
15	A Journey Home	Pg 117
16	Cate	Pg 127
17	The Preacher	Pg 139
18	Keena	Pg 155
19	Riders of the Range	Pg 173
20	City by the Lake	Pg 185
21	Fire in the Hole	Pg 193
22	Wilds of Wisconsin	Pg 209
23	Quarrians	Pg 221
24	A Final Letter	Pg 231
25	Atwood Center	Pg 241
26	A Queen	Pg 251
27	His Will	Pg 259

Matthew J Krengel

ACKNOWLEDGMENTS

The Ancient Mayans. In my imagination, all they had wrong was the date.

Matthew J Krengel

1 Category Six?

Black rain clouds driven by one hundred mile-an-hour winds tore at central Guatemala dumping torrents of rain on two desperate men stranded in a remote valley. Flashes of verdant jungles looked down on them through the curtains of water blowing so hard that it nearly fell sideways. Rain pounded the ground around them and soaked them both to the skin, their hair plastered flat against their scalps and cold winds tore at their wet clothes. The older man stood on a small outcropping of stone staring at the rising rivers of water racing below his perch. Half a dozen steps in front of him a younger looking man knelt by the river and dipped his hands in the raging serpent to rinse away the mud of a recent fall. Not that the difference in age was really that dramatic but one showed his age much more than the other.

"Wait! I think I see something!" Dr James Kaning cried.

Dr. Alan Stewart glanced up from his knelling perch beside the water. Already the river was beginning to crest its banks and fill small dips and crevasses along the narrow valley floor. Before long it would completely wash out the surrounding hillsides and the danger would be worse as tons of mud entered the roaring serpent.

"What is it, Kaning?" Alan screamed. Despite the cry his voice barely carried as a small sound to James where he stood shading his eyes against the rain. The roar of the thunder and wind crashed constantly making communication nearly impossible.

"I think I see a hill sticking out of the jungles behind us." Excitedly James motioned to the south, there the jungle waited dark and steaming. Even worse now the torrents of rain were beginning to eat away at the roots of ancient trees. Dangerous creaks and groans filled the air as the earth protested under the violent assault.

"We need to keep moving," replied Alan. He rose to his feet and walked to where James stood still stared away to the south. "We just came from the direction. I don't remember seeing any hills in that part of the jungle."

"All the same, I am telling you there is something out there. Look! Follow my finger." James said again. He looked down and yelped as the water began to lap at their feet. It was rising quickly now and soon would sweep them away unless they moved.

"Fine, let's just move before we are caught here in the open and swept down river." Alan growled. With his explosive temper and matching red hair and beard he was a barrel of a man who loved fighting almost as much as he loved archeology. Some had criticized him over the years as having a darker side but he was as brilliant a mind as ever existed in the field of archeology. A tattered ball cap that offered a bit of protection from the wind and rain hid his short-cropped hair.

James nodded as he hopped up the slope and out of the reach of the water.

"If I ever find those guides there will be hell to pay!" Alan growled in frustration as they started out. They both scrambled up a slight slope that gave a bit of protection from the raging torrents below.

James nodded his head and began trotting towards the line of trees marking the edge of the jungle. His sandy blond hair lay matted to his head and he was constantly wiping away the small rivulets of water as they wandered down his face.

"Where next," asked Alan. Overhead the jungle canopy closed together giving the two men a tiny bit of protection from the waves of rain. Yet even through the thick foliage they still felt the intense winds of Hurricane Erik, as the massive category six hurricane unleashed its full fury against the eastern coasts of Guatemala and Mexico. He still didn't understand how a hurricane could crop up this suddenly and completely out of season. Still there it was, bigger than anything the gulf area had seen in decades. Alan looked up in irritation, they had both watched the weather reports before leaving Guatemala City. The forecasts showed only a small storm tracking much further south but nothing like this.

"You know this is just the leading edge of the storm. When the main body strikes land it is going to sweep this entire jungle clean of anything without a hundred year root system." James cried. Together they scrambled across patches of ferns and skirted the trunks of ancient trees. Already the ground was becoming a morass of pools and thick patches of mud that tore at their shoes and threatened to swallow them whole into the heart of the jungle. "We have to find shelter, hopefully underground shelter."

"There!" cried Alan. "Over there is your hill!" He pointed to the right of where they stood as a constant barrage of lightening shook the sky and the corresponding thunder rumbled across the ground. "What will it be the wind or the water?"

"Not a moment too soon," replied James. He glanced over his shoulder and the sight that greeted his eyes spurred him on to faster movement. Behind them a raging wall of water had entered the jungle and roared at them like a living thing. "Climb!" he screamed. He would rather take his chance with the wind then the torrents of water heading towards them.

Alan did not need to be told twice; he threw his body at muddy slopes of the hill and clawed his way up behind James. Roots and branches flew as he tore at the ground reaching for anything that would offer even the slightest bit of aid in climbing. Even though Alan was three years younger than James he lacked the older man's natural athleticism. Together they raced for their lives against the approaching flood water. Alan was less than half way up the hillside when he began to lose his footing and slip backwards. Desperately he threw himself forward and lay gasping for air against the mud. Bits of plants and tree roots flowed down the hillside and lodged against his body adding to the difficulty of keeping his grip.

"Come on, Alan!" James had reached the relative safety of a large stone outcropping and he leaned over the edge. Stretching as far as he dared he reached out to the stranded Dr Stewart and called out encouragingly. His grip was tenuous on the roots but he gripped it as tightly as he could as he tried to help his friend.

"I am coming you pathetic twit," grunted Alan. It wasn't that he didn't appreciate the older man's enthusiasm, but he was in no mood for any encouragement at the moment. In truth it had been James decision to push on even when their guides had insisted they turn back and seek higher ground. Now with the river tugging at his legs, he found that he was truly beginning to hate the smiling face looking down at him.

"Come on, Alan. I think I found some shelter." James called again then his hand reached down and caught Alan's outstretched arms. With a quick pull he heaved the younger scientist over the edge of the rock and together they sat breathing heavily for more than a minute.

"Well this is fun," Alan grumbled as he gasped for air his arms shaking from the effort of climbing against the flow of mud.

"I think the river is subsiding just a little," James said. He pointed down six feet to where the muddy water receded back into the jungle ever so slightly. From their perch James figured they had managed to climb about half of the sloping base of a wide hill. Above and around them rose a tangle of vines, heavy undergrowth and a scattering of stunted trees.

"Well, what now," Alan grumbled. He glared out at the water as it swirled around the trees and reached towards them again. Contrary to what James thought of the wind he still viewed the water as their biggest threat.

"Let's work our way higher, this slope has some familiar looking features," James said. He skirted the rock face that looked down over them and began to climb over the stones sticking out of the undergrowth. The higher they climbed the more stone they found and the more uniform the hill became. It was soon obvious to both of them that this was not a hill but an undiscovered temple, and despite their precarious circumstance, they both wondered if this was the beginning of a much larger complex.

"It is definitely man-made!" cried Alan when they reached the summit. High overhead black clouds piled up to the east and cast their ominous gaze down at the two men. The powerful storm clouds unleashed winds that threatened to send both men tumbling away.

"We cannot stay here either," shouted James. He raised a hand to shield his face from the gusts and the bits of sand and dirt that swirled about.

Alan nodded in agreement, after one last look around the small plateau they scrambled down the south side seeking a more permanent shelter. Thankfully the moment they stepped off the summit the wind subsided a bit and they were able to take a few minutes to examine the hillside. The stones on this side were more obviously placed by human hands but the thick covering of vines would have easily hidden it from human eyes.

"Over there!" James cried in excitement. He pointed across the hillside where the ground formed a slight hollow protected by what was obviously a manmade wall formed of limestone.

They scrambled towards the opening as the rain strengthened and the winds began to howl across the hill once again. Two minutes of slipping and sliding finally brought them into the shadow of the limestone cleft and James collapsed to the ground. Next to him Alan struggled to regain his breath and calm the trembling in his legs.

"Well what now!" cried Alan when he finally found enough breath and energy to be able to talk again? Against all odds the wind seemed to have strengthened again and they were unable to even poke their heads out from behind the stone wall for fear of catching debris in the eyes or face.

"I don't know," James shouted back. He shrugged as he turned to examine the flat section of the hill; the limestone wall protected a second structure built into the side of the mountain. At some point in the past a third wall had existed but it had succumbed to the forces of time and erosion. The only thing that remained was a tumble of stones that fanned out from the base of the wall and spread across the nearby hillside. On the section of wall built into the hill was a single word etched deeply into the soft stone and thankfully it had withstood the effects of time.

"What does this say, Alan?" James pointed to the word. "I have not seen this type of hieroglyph before."

"Well, for one thing remember that the Mayan language is more of a logographic system of writing not a hieroglyph system. With more than a thousand known glyphs it is possible that there are more than a few that no one knows." Alan huffed. He shuffled over to where James was rolling his eyes and leaned close to the wall. He ran his fingers over the stone in an effort to clear away the few remaining bits of roots and dirt. He was silent for nearly five minutes before he cleared his throat and spoke. "I think it is a variation of glyph that most commonly stands for the idea of 'enter here'."

"Well that doesn't make any sense." James leaned close to the wall and examined the crevasses between the stones. "These are fitted together so closely I can't tell if there is anything behind them or not." He pushed and poked at the wall trying to find a way to remove the stones.

A sudden roar startled both of them and they turned just in time to see a tree rocket by their small shelter and cut a massive furrow in the hill below them. Bits of rock flew into the air and a massive tumble of bigger rocks rolled away. James's light brown coat tugged against his body as the wind intensified again and the suction pulled at their bodies trying to rip them free of the hill and send them to their deaths.

"We have to find a better shelter!" Alan shouted again, without warning his hat flew off his head and disappeared into the maelstrom, a victim of the horrible winds.

James nodded and he flattened his back against the wall under the glyphs. Then he felt it when he put his hand against the rocks, the pull of the wind. He slid his hand along the wall to a wider crack and his face split into a smile.

"There is a way to enter!" shouted James. Frantically he pushed and shoved on the stones searching for one that might be looser then the surrounding ones. Alan stared at him for a second and then joined him in the frantic search. They searched the entire wall twice when James's hand fell against a bit of root sticking out between two stones near the ground. In irritation he grabbed the root and pulled with all of his might. Surprisingly he felt the root begin to give then slowly and smoothly it gave way and the two stones on either side slid out and fell away, revealing a dark opening.

"We found it!" James cried as he grabbed Alan's coat. The hole that opened in the stones was only big enough for one of them to fit in at once and James dove headfirst into the darkness. Immediately he reached back and grabbed Alan's outstretched hands and helped him into the relative calm of a small anti-chamber.

"Think we are safe now?" Alan shouted. He immediately broke into a cold laugh as his voice echoed in the room. They had been standing in the storm for so long their ears still rang with the force of the wind. Slowly, the ringing subsided and they were able to once again speak in normal voices. "One good hit and we are still dead."

"I don't know," replied James in a more normal tone. Suddenly the hillside shook again as something large struck the hill and a shower of dirt fell from the ceiling. On a sudden inspiration James dug into the cargo pocket of his brown pants and to his delight found that his battered MAG light was still secured in the pocket. He pulled the flashlight out and clicked the button on the handle, they both smiled in relief when a thin pencil of light lit the dim room.

"Amazing," muttered Alan. The room was approximately ten feet square with a vaulted ceiling of heavy limestone blocks fitted together at angles to support the weight of the hillside. The ancient Mayans had crafted the blocks together with perfect precision but what was even more amazing was the painted gold mantel and posts that marked the entrance to the next chamber.

"I have never heard of the Mayans sheathing the entrance of a temple with gold. This must be a temple of some importance." James muttered under his breath. Alan grunted at him but continued to examine the glyphs painted above the door.

"Shine the light over here a bit more," Alan demanded. Never one to mince words, he did not even turn to see if James would do what he wanted. The younger archeologist tapped his foot in irritation as he waited for James to comply with his order.

James sighed and turned the flashlight so it shown over Alan's shoulder, the runes painted above the wall were red and black in keeping with Mayan tradition. Beyond the physical makeup of the paint and the etching James was unable to decipher most of the glyphs so he waited while Alan muttered to himself.

2 Temple of Time

"Temple of Time Eternal," muttered Alan. "Well roughly translated anyway. Some of the glyphs seem to be earlier versions of more commonly used ones from the Mayan Classical era."

"So do you think it predates the Olmec's?" James asked. It was hard for him to believe that a civilization could have predated the most ancient of the known Meso-American peoples. Even with modern equipment and research techniques little was understood about how the Olmec's had influenced later empires.

"I don't know, it might. I have never heard of anything described as a temple dedicated to time though. We could be on the verge of the greatest archeological discovery of the modern age, James." Alan's voice was filled with an awe and reverence reserved for the most important of occasions. He ran his hand over the paint slowly; his hand shook slightly as the realization settled on him that they might never be able to publish anything about it.

James nearly dropped his flashlight when Alan said his first name. After four years in the field and countless hours spent toiling under blazing suns, this was the first time he had heard the younger man use his first name.

"Shall we go down the steps? I don't think the local authorities will be in any position to complain for a while," James asked. As if to emphasis his point a terribly loud crash shook the entire hill as again something smashed into the hidden temple.

"It would probably be safer deeper underground," Alan agreed with a sarcastic snort.

James used his small flashlight to check the steps, and then he tentatively stepped out onto the stones. Bits of dust and dirt filtered down from the roof as the hillside shook again but the limestone walls and ceiling held strong.

"Look, there are some torches here on the wall. Let me see if I can light one." Alan removed a torch from the stone cradle in the wall and reached into his right front pants pocket. From the wet material he removed an antique lighter; carefully he struck the lighter and held it close to the top of the torch. The wood sputtered for a moment but finally caught. When they each held a lit torch and carried a spare James clicked off the flashlight and they proceeded slowly down the steps. Their breath came in short and excited gasps as they examined the walls and talked excitedly about the designs etched into each stone.

It took them thirty-four steps to reach the bottom of the stairs and the sounds of the storm far above had now faded completely. Silence closed in around them broken only by the sputters of the torches and their own footsteps.

"I still think I hear running water," James muttered. He cocked his head to the side straining to pick out the sounds echoing in the tunnel. "Maybe I'm wrong."

"No, I hear it too." Alan crossed through the next door that was unmarked and then he skidded to a halt so fast that James bumped into him and nearly dropped his torch.

"Amazing!" Alan muttered. He glanced back as James grumbled behind him.

James fumbled with his torch for a moment and then he looked up and froze. Above them in the flickering light of the torch a perfect painting of the night sky stared back at them. Each star flickered and glowed in the sudden light of the torches like it contained a life of its own. The craftsmanship of the interior of the temple was beyond perfect as was the painting. Never before had anything of this scope been discovered anywhere in Central or South America.

"How did they…" James's voice faded off as his mind struggled to process the sheer scope of the representation of the universe. His mind spun until he finally managed to tear his eyes from the ceiling and examine the room that stretched out before them. Two massive bowls filled with a liquid bracketed the door on each side. Out of curiosity he dripped a finger into the liquid and then lifted it to his nose.

"Oil," James muttered. On a whim he brought his torch down until the flame touched the surface of the oil. He was rewarded with a bluish light as the flame spread across the surface until the oil pot was completely ablaze. He noticed immediately that the flame seemed drawn towards a small hole drilled into the wall. The small bits of smoke that rolled off the flame were immediately drawn into the hole and disappeared. Apparently the ancient Mayans had devised a system to siphon off the smoke from these lamps.

Simply amazing," Alan repeated again. Without so much as a glance at his partner he dipped his torch into the other lamp and then snuffed the torch out on a nearby pile of

13

sand. Once it was out he simply dropped it to the ground and it was gone from his mind.

"To think that the Mayans were able to construct such a room and then paint the ceiling into such an accurate representation of the night sky is mind boggling," James agreed. He snuffed out his own torch and then turned in a slow circle examining the entire observatory. Nearly sixty feet across and at least forty feet wide, the floor stepped down at regular intervals. Near the center of the room sat a circle of chairs each made of carved stone and etched with myriads of glyphs and pictographs.

"Ha-ha," Suddenly Alan turned and grabbed James around the shoulders and began a wild dance. "We are famous. More than famous, our names will be spoken in every college room and university campus across the world." His face was wild with the anticipation of the glory that would be heaped on their heads.

Abruptly he released his grip on James and rushed down the steps to the circle of chairs. When he arrived he dashed about examining each for but a second. James shook his head at the abrupt change in his normally reserved partner. Still, James's smile widened until he could no longer hold back the laughter. Unsure of what to look at first he decided to join Alan at the circle of thrones.

"Are they thrones? Are they observation chairs made to look at the night sky?" Alan was muttering. He walked around each of the chairs, examining them in the steady light of the oil lamps. "Look, here is a chair dedicated to Venus." Alan ran his fingers over the glyphs and then finally slipped into the chair. Carefully he leaned back letting his body rest fully into the throne, a loud click echoed in the room and slowly the back of the throne hinged back.

James watched with his heart pounding in his throat, mentally he ordered himself to calm down. They were on uncharted waters here, the ancients who designed this temple may have left traps to protect their devices.

"James, this is amazing. I am staring directly at the painting of Venus on the ceiling." He raised his hand and pointed at the distant star. "Go ahead, try one out."

James walked around the circle carefully looking at each of the dominate glyphs carved into the top of the chairs. Finally he chose one that he thought was named for meteors. Slowly he slipped into the chair and waited for it to slide into the reclined position. Instead another loud click echoed through the room and a massive round stone set into the floor in the middle of the chairs began to rise into the air.

"What did you do?" Alan nearly shouted as his chair came back to the upright position.

"I don't know. I didn't do anything but sit down." James shot back. He jumped out of the chair but it did not stop moving and the circular stone continued rising so he stepped to the side and watched.

The central stone rose until it was chest height. Then it stopped and the room fell silent again. Carefully James slipped back into the chair and leaned back. "I am not really looking at anything, just a space out past where Pluto would be."

"Alan, do you have your lighter yet?" James asked. He leaned forward but was careful not to take his weight off the chair.

"Yes, why?" Alan responded as he dug in his pocket.

"Toss it to me."

"Alright, but don't break it. This lighter is one of a kind." Alan grumbled as he took the gold-sheathed lighter from his pocket and tossed it across the stone to James. He glared at the other man until the lighter landed safely in his outstretched hand.

"I won't and stop being such an old woman," laughed James. "We are in the middle of the greatest discovery in modern archeology and you're worried about a seventy year old lighter."

James flipped the lighter open and worked the mechanism until an inch tall flame erupted from the metal casing. Carefully he leaned forward and slipped the lighter under an open space below the top of the round stone. He was rewarded a moment later with the hissing sound of burning oil, then he nearly dropped the precious lighter as both of their seats began to recline even further. This time though the two chairs swiveled towards the door where they entered.

"What in the ..." Alan voice faded off as a twinkle of tiny lights was suddenly projected at the ceiling in the furthest corner. In contrast to the brilliant white of the stars that filled the night sky these pinpricks of light were red in color. With a lurch the chairs and the round stone between them began to slowly rotate creating the illusion that the angry swarm of lights was moving across the sky.

"Just what was written on that chair," asked Alan as he watched the red dots close on the circle of stars that represented Sol. A deep sense of dread began to fill his spirit as all of the dooms day prophecies began to fill his mind.

"I think it had a date and the glyph for meteors on it." James said in awe. Exactly one minute later the swarm of red lights had converged on the third star from the sun, after touching the earth they winked out of existence.

Both men sat silently while their chairs returned to the upright position and the fire winked out from under the round stone. With a loud grind the central stone sank back into the ground and the circle of chairs returned to their original position.

They both stood up immediately, not wanting to know if the machinery could repeat the sequence again. Alan rushed to the chair James had sat on and began to decipher the runes etched across the wide limestone block at the top. He stood muttering under his breath as his fingers traced the ancient carvings.

James turned away and examined the room from where he stood. It was then he noticed that spread out at regular intervals around the perimeter stood a series of carved statues. Their faces were locked into fierce snarls and murderous expressions but the thing that drew his attention most were the fist sized stones that had been set into the chest of each of the warriors directly over their hearts.

"Alan, have you ever seen Mayan carvings with stones set into the place where their heart should be?" James asked quietly. When Alan failed to answer he glanced over at him and seeing that the younger man was completely engrossed with the glyphs, he started up the steps towards the nearest carving. When he arrived he shuddered at the vicious look on the creatures face. What at first he thought was a human face turned hideous the closer he got. The half man looking creature had bulbous eyes and pair of small slits where the nose should have been, the carving had one arm stretched down almost to its knees and carried a wicked serrated sword.

Tearing his eyes from the creatures face James reached out carefully to touch the dimly glowing stone over its heart.

3 The Codex

"It's today's date and the symbol is not just for a single meteor but a whole shower of meteors." Alan said suddenly. His face paled visibly, "Could it be that there really is something to the hysteria surrounding last year?" His mind raced as he thought about the possibility that the ancients had known something was going to happen and they had made the effort to warn those who came after.

James's hand jerked back from the stone he had just about touched. He turned slowly, almost like he was waking from a dream and stared at Dr Stewart. Suddenly he shook his head and reached up with both hands to rub his face. He felt like he was in a trance as his mind struggled through the fog that filled it.

"Are you alright?" Alan asked.

"Yes, I... Well I am not sure. What was that you said?" Again the concern was uncustomary and it took James by surprise.

"The glyphs represent the Mayan concept of catastrophe from above and this series of marks here stands for today's date. Think of it James, an exact reason as to why the Mayan's ended their calendar in the year two thousand twelve," Alan explained as he shook his head. "The only difference is that the real date is listed in this temple as two thousand thirteen."

"I always thought that there would be a different explanation to why they ended their calendar last year." James turned and stared at the statues which in turned glared down at them. "I mean, we have all watched the History Channel specials about the end of the world. Just for fun last year I read three books about all the evils that the conspiracy theorists dreamed up."

"Then, of course, you have the less reliable sources like the writings of Nostradamus. There are hundreds of legends and stories about major catastrophes and for some reason they all center around last year," finished Alan. His voice was patronizing as he grinned at James. "I thought since we made it though we were safe. And you think it was all true. The world does end this year and more specifically today."

"Well, what do you think we should do?" James asked. Finally he tore his gaze from the heart stone and pushed back the cloud of confusion that threatened to wash him away. He stared at Alan and wondered at his lighthearted tone.

"What can we do?" Alan retorted. "Sit back and enjoy our discovery until something big takes out this temple." Shrugging his shoulders Alan turned away from the circle of chairs and began examining the ceiling again. Almost listlessly he muttered to himself. "Greatest discovery of the century and it happens on the day the world dies."

"Maybe it won't happen. Maybe the Mayans were wrong," said James hopefully. He found his eyes continually straying to the massive gemstone, his finger twitched with the want to touch the stone. Despite his words he could not understand if Alan was mocking him or simply resigned to whatever fate had in store for them.

"Wrong," Alan scoffed. "How could the people who built this room and painted a perfect representation of the night sky. They are not off. These ancients managed to construct a device capable of warning anyone who finds this temple and is smart enough or lucky enough to activate it. And you think that they might have been wrong? Look here, this is the Haab solar calendar here." Alan exploded. "You know what this stands for in Mayan lore." He pointed to a nearby calendar chiseled into the wall.

James nodded, "Eighteen months with twenty days in each. Along with a five-day period called Wayeb that was considered a time of great evil. The ancient Mayans would go out of their way to avoid trouble. According to Foster's Handbook to Life in the Ancient Mayan World they had a whole list of customs and rituals to avoid the evil spirits; it was assumed that these actions would help ward off troubled times."

They were silent for a few minutes until Alan finally spoke, "Do you know what today is in the Haab calendar, if you take into account the partial day lost each year? It is the first day of Wayeb, the day the barriers between our world and the spirit world dissolve according to the Mayans. This is the day the world as we know it ends."

James's shoulders slumped as he listened to the words, deep inside he knew that he would never see his family again. Sullenly he began to wander the room, the masterpiece above his head held no interest for him anymore. His wife back home in St Cloud, Minnesota and their son, they were the only people that held his thoughts now. He knew there was no way to get home quickly and the thought of not seeing his family again struck him hard.

As he wandered he found himself counting the smaller chairs scattered in an orderly fashion around the sunken floor.

There were fifty-two seats total in the chamber marking the exact number of years in the Mayan Calendar Round. James stopped to examine what he assumed was the last seat in the sequence when something caught his eye. Tucked in the corner of the deep shadow cast by the two lamps he noticed something, it was the edge of a bound volume sitting between the seat and the ancient arm rest waiting for the next person to come and find it.

With shaking hands James reached out and retrieved the book covered in Mayan glyphs.

"Alan," he muttered. When there was no answer he called louder. "ALAN!"

"What, what do you want! Can't you even let me die in peace," exploded the younger scientist. When he saw what James held his voice trailed off, again a flash of curiosity emerged in his eyes.

"It is a codex, one never seen before. Look, the glyph on the top is the same as over the mantle to the temple. Roughly translated it says Book of Time Eternal," James said as he turned to look at Alan.

James's heart pounded in his chest as he carried the ancient book to the circle of marked thrones. Gently he laid the volume on the stone and they bent over it together. The pages crackled with age but held together and with bated breath they began to read what was written on the pages.

"This is amazing; this book is literally a user manual for this temple. Look, here it says that in the time of greatest terror the heartstone with protect you. I wonder what that means."

"I think I know," muttered James. He stood and walked to where the hideous statue still glared at them. "Here it is, set in the chest of these guardians." He stepped back and examined the pair of statues before the burning lamps.

Besides being hideously ugly the statues each held one hand up in the air with the palm pointed towards the ceiling. Standing there looking at the guardian James suddenly had an idea.

"Alan..." he started when a tremendous roar shook the temple and the ground below their feet bucked wildly.

"It's happening!" Alan cried. He raced back to the stairs and disappeared up the steps not waiting to see if James would follow or not. Suddenly he didn't want to be underground and have the life crushed from him by falling stones.

"Wait, Alan," James cried. He spared the statue one last look and then raced after Alan up the dark steps. He fell twice going up the stairs as the limestone shook beneath his feet. Outside the temple they skidded to a halt and stared up at the sky. Amazingly, overhead the sun had broken through the clouds and offered a bit of warmth to the troubled world. Despite the sunshine above their heads, black clouds walled them on all sides, but the world around them was calm and at peace. It may have been a false peace but it was peace for a brief moment.

"We are in the eye of the hurricane," muttered James. All about a terrible calm descended and the silence sent a shiver up his spine.

"Look!" Alan cried suddenly his voice filled with terror and rage. "Behold the end of the world."

James looked up and stared, high in the sky a single blazing trail marked the beginning of the end. A massive ball of fire burning across the sky heralded the coming destruction. Then the first meteor was joined by a second at a slightly different angle.

"God help us all," James sank to his knees, as the two fiery trails suddenly became a dozen. Soon after the dozen multiplied until it seemed that the entire sky was filled with fire. Then the winds began to pick up and the dark clouds covered the sky again..

4 Burning Sky

They watched the impending doom for what seemed to James like an eternity but in reality only two or three minutes. Without warning huge drops of rain began to fall as around them and the hurricane reestablished its hold. Overhead the black clouds cut all view of the meteor firestorm, and then as they watched a single meteor broke through the clouds and raced across the sky. It sank quickly as it disappeared beyond the jungle to the north.

"We should get back inside, either we get blown off the hillside by the hurricane or die when a meteor strikes the temple. I would rather not know when I am going to die," James cried over the howling winds.

"Wait, I want to see what happens!" Alan cried. He stubbornly clung to the limestone and stared out across the valley but the thick vegetation blocked off where the meteor was about to impact.

Thump.....

James almost snickered when he heard the barely audible sound of the space debris striking terra. The laugh stopped a moment later when a towering column of earth and trees rocketed into the horizon far to the north.

"Get inside, get inside now!" James screamed. He dove for the opening in the temple door and rolled away to make room for his partner. A moment later, Alan struggled through the space in the wall and together they raced down the stairs hoping the hillside would shelter them from the coming shockwave. They made it half way down the steps when the temple complex began to shudder. Screaming in terror both men clung to whatever they could find as the steps buckled and shook under their feet.

"Get back into the central chamber!"

James nodded and pulled himself down the steps on his knees as an ominous rumble grew deep in the earth and vibrated through the walls. Behind them James heard a large chunk of stone crash to the ground and bits of dirt and dust sprayed across both of them.

"What now?" James cried as they scrambled into the central chamber, the walls shook and buckled as tremors traveled through the earth around them. Thankfully the construction of the temple was sound and walls absorbed the impact.

"I don't know. We wait for the entire chamber to collapse." Alan's words had just faded when the stones supporting much of the ceiling above the stairs gave into the stresses tearing at the earth and collapsed with a roar of dust that nearly extinguished their two lamps.

James looked about racking his mind for something that would allow them to survive. He turned to the guardian statue next to them and examined the heartstone. Again he felt the overwhelming urge to reach out and touch the stone. "It isn't like anyone is going to be around to complain," he muttered under his breath. Finally he gave into the urge and placed his hand against the stone.

Click

"What the..." James exclaimed. An oval shaped stone came free of the statues chest cavity and fell into his hands. He juggled the stone as he tried to get a firm grip on the polished surface. Finally he wrapped his fingers around the stone and raised it up so that he could look into its depths. Deep inside the stone it seemed like something moved, curling back and forth, trapped inside the surface of the stone.

Suddenly a massive tremor shook the earth and the stones holding the chamber together swayed violently. James looked up at the ceiling and prayed fervently that it would hold together. As he stared up, his eyes traveled up the statues arm and came to rest on the upheld hand.

"Well, why not," muttered James as his mind worked feverishly. Carefully he reached up and slipped the stone into the hand of the statue. The moment the heartstone touched the stone a brilliant shaft of ruby light flashed out and struck the round stone in the center of the chamber.

"Alan!" James cried. He shouted to Dr Stewart as he sprinted around the top of the room and skidded to a halt in front of the next statue.

"What now!"

"The stones! Get the stones from their chests and place it in their hands."

Alan stared blankly at the brilliant red light in surprise and then nodded. He jumped to his feet and jogged around the room in the opposite direction.

James turned back to his own statue and paused as he stared at the carving, this time the statue was that of a woman. With a fine facial structure and high cheekbones the statue reminded him of drawings made of Cleopatra's sarcophagus, except for the odd pointed shaping of her ears. His hands shook as he removed the stone and looked at it briefly before putting it atop the outstretched hand. This time the stone was bluish; tearing his eyes from it he reached up and slipped it into her waiting hand.

"It's not working!" Alan cried from across the room. He had placed the stone into the statues hands and it fit perfectly but nothing happened.

James turned and looked across the room and saw that the statue where Alan was standing had also failed to light up. Growling in irritation James turned back to the statue and stared at it, what was different about this one from the last he asked himself over and over? Suddenly the ground shook again and clouds of dust began to filter out of the walls making dancing shadows in the light of the two torches. *The light* he thought as his eyes flashed back to where the torches they had lit still burned brightly.

"The torches!" James screamed. Shaking his head he turned and sprinted back to where they had put down the torches they carried into the chamber. "Get your torch and light the rest of the lamps!" James grabbed the unlit torch and pushed it into the flames, he held it there until it was again burning brightly and then hurried to the next set of metal lamps.

Alan nodded as his mind made the same connection at nearly the same time. Two minutes later eighteen bronze lamps blazed merrily adding their light together until the room shown brilliantly. Nine shafts of light blazed down towards the round stone and the hair on James's arms and neck stood on end from the feelings of power filling the room. It was like standing outside during a lightning storm, it felt to him like the room was alive. The final figure reminded him of every statue he had ever seen of the ancient Mayans; carefully he took the earth colored stone from the guardian.

The moment the stone touched the palm of the statues hand a brilliant blast of dark brown light erupted and joined the rest. Both men turned as the shaft of light struck the stone. The moment the light touched the stone it spun in a circle. Around and around it went like a child's toy top. With each revolution the stone moved higher and higher until it finally began to slow. The stone stood nearly ten feet up in the air when it finally ground to a halt revealing another set of stairs.

"Amazing!"

James just shook his head unsure of what to say, his mind reeled as he tried to imagine the sheer amount of skilled engineering that had gone into the construction of this chamber. Tentatively he walked down and approached the stairs. He jumped when the stone clicked one last time. The brilliant shafts of light were now striking some type of mirror system that reflected the beams down into the earth and lit the path for them. Around them the hill took another direct hit from something big and shook violently before calming again.

"What have we got to lose? Might as well see where it all leads." James turned and looked at Alan for confirmation that he felt the same. "We may not survive if we don't get further underground."

"Might as well," agreed Alan.

James shoved his head between the posts and looked down into the massive hole in the ground. Curiously the nine beams of light did not combine when they were focused down into the ground. They stayed separate as they disappeared into the depths of the earth. A set of wooden steps led down for about twenty feet until the ended in an earthen wall.

"Wooden stairs but they look solid even after all these years."

Alan nodded, "Let's keep moving. If this structure takes a direct hit from a meteor we may never find out what is at the bottom."

James nodded but then grimaced as he stepped out onto the first step. The ancient wood creaked and groaned but held firm when he put his weight on it. The next twenty steps were the longest of his life as each of the wooden planks protested. When he finally put his feet back on the solid stone again he leaned on the wall and tried to calm is mind and body.

"I made it, come on over," James said. Over the pounding of his heart he tried to sound nonchalant. All around them the hole in the ground appeared to be laid out in a perfect circle. It disappeared down into the ground until the rainbow of lights was lost from sight. The steps circled the outside supported by stone abutments.

"My goodness it goes down forever." Alan's voice shook with fear as he clung to the outer wall. "I hate heights." He leaned out and glanced over the edge but his face went white and he hastily pulled back.

"Stick next to the wall," James advised. With a deep sigh he led off and began down the long series of steps.

Thirty minutes later James checked his watch for the fifth time and then leaned out and looked down. In the distance far below them he thought he saw something but was unsure.

"I think I see something." James turned to Alan and clapped him on the shoulder with a brilliant smile. "You're almost there."

"Thank god. Much more of this and I am going to lose my mind." Alan's voice held a tinge of panic in it and his eyes rolled wildly.

Fifteen minutes later they stepped off the last of the stairs and took a deep breath of the stale air. Alan fell to his knees and leaned with his shoulder against the wall, he took a deep breath and willed his shaking hands to stop their tremors.

5 Path to Power

James felt the earth shake under his feet once and his heart stopped in his chest as the separate beams of light flickered for a moment. Neither man drew a breath until the light steadied, with a sigh of relief they began to examine their surroundings. Curiously the area was free of dust and the path into the earth looked to be man-made. They were in a round chamber with limestone walls, a second round mirror channeled the lights into a hallway that the compass in James's watch told him was north.

The tunnel drove in a straight line for nearly four hundred yards before stopping. The ceiling was about ten feet in the air and it was about eight feet wide. If it had once been a natural cave whoever had built the temple and stairs had also sanded and polished the stone of the walls and ceiling until they were smooth.

"That the Mayan's managed to make a rainbow of light is a technological marvel in itself. But this is beyond amazing. The light does not seem to have lost any of its intensity despite the distance it has traveled," said Alan. Now that they had left the spiraling stairs he was beginning to regain control over his emotions and his mind.

The tunnel ended in a massive underground room. The first thing James saw when they entered the door was a third round mirror once again diffusing the rainbow of lights and sending them streaming out in nine different directions. Their eyes followed the beams as they flowed across the room and impacted at ten points across the chamber. James turned and looked up at the wall behind them, the beam of red light traveled up the wall to a point about twenty feet up where it entered a second crystal. The beam then angled up to the center of the ceiling and entered what looked to James to be a massive faceted gemstone. As the beam of light left the gemstone it shot straight down from there and ended on the floor between two objects too far away for James to make them out. It was a brilliant shaft of light that combined all of the colors of the spectrum into two brilliant beams of power.

"What are those?" Alan pointed at the distant spot where the beams of light were converging. Two silvery objects reflected bits of light back at them.

"I don't know," James shrugged. Ever since he entered the chamber the hair on the back of his neck was standing on end and the urge to run away washed over him so strongly that he nearly bolted. "I, uhh... think we should go find out?"

"Well, we have nothing better to do. The ancient Mayans built this for a reason. I think we should go find out what that reason is," Alan grunted. His red hair was a bit wild and he tugged at his beard in unrestrained excitement.

James's heart wilted in his chest as he thought about crossing the stone floor. Even the rainbow of light, which before had seemed friendly to him, now took on an ominous hue.

Alan walked quickly, the excitement he felt showing in his stride. Now that the stairs were behind him, his confidence returned in full force. Even his arrogance seemed to have returned as he turned and glared at James, "Come on, move it."

"Coming," said James. He forced his body to move forward and follow his colleague. When he finally arrived at the device his fear took a back seat to his curiosity. Alan stood silently with his head cocked to the side staring at it.

"How?"

"I don't know," Alan replied to the question in irritation. "No one in the world knows."

"But........"

"I don't know, alright," repeated the archeologist. "It's not possible, alright. But that being said, here we are confronted with something that is not possible." Alan shot him a look that told him not to interrupt again and turned back to the odd device.

They were both silent for nearly five minutes as they examined the object in front of them. To James it resembled the feathered headpiece that was carved into hundreds of murals across Central and South America. The difference was that this one had two metal pillars next to it with indents where a person could place their hands. Four of the light beams combined into a single beam and ended in a crystal set in the top of the right pillar. To their amazement the beams of light combined to nearly black, an almost malevolent look while the beam that gathered together and fed into the left side was pure white. James's spirit leaped in his chest when he looked at the left beam. In the middle, a pale round circle of light marked the ninth beam and beckoned them to step forward.

"The metal looks like steel but it isn't," said Alan. He knelt next to the pillar on the right and leaned forward until his nose almost touched the surface.

"How can you tell?" queried James as he took a step closer to the left pillar. Carefully he reached out and touched the surface of the pillar, the metal yielded under his touch but when he removed his finger the metal flowed back into place.

"Can I take that question back?" James said with a chuckle. "I have heard of metals that will heal themselves but nothing like this."

Alan snorted but decided to ignore the poor attempt at humor. He eyes were continually drawn to the black beam of light, in his mind the blackness was reflected. He always dreamed of wielding power beyond the world of academia. Control was what he craved and a small voice in his mind told him that the device would give him that control, but only if he could get rid of James. That was his weakness, James was born into a famous family with more wealth then most people only dreamed about. He was the one that stood in Alan's way. There was no reason to the madness that took his mind, only the want to control the lives of everything and everyone around him.

"What is it?" James asked suddenly. Nervously he shifted when he noticed that Alan was glaring at him with hatred blazing in his eyes. He knew his fellow academic was a bit unstable but his genius made up for the moments of odd behavior.

"What? Nothing I was just lost in thought," replied Alan. He tore his gaze away and forced the dark thought away from him.

"Do you think we should try it?" James asked.

"Yes, of course." Alan snorted at the imbecilic question. "The world above us is ending, we have nothing to lose."

James nodded, suddenly he had an idea and he slipped the codex from the makeshift pack he carried over his shoulder. Carefully he unfolded the pages until he found what he was searching for.

"I knew I had seen this device somewhere. Look, it is drawn out here in the codex," James said excitedly. He bent over the book and squinted at the glyphs. "If I am reading this correctly it says located in the Chamber of Power deep underneath is the power of the ancients. The power to raise great buildings and the power to bring those buildings down. The power to bend men's minds and to break them their bodies. After that it just says use wisely for even the unjust may partake."

"Interesting," muttered Alan. He stared at the device without blinking.

"I can't read the rest of it. The glyphs are un-translated in our language."

Suddenly Alan swept the headpiece off the stand and slid it over his head, "History does not record the actions of the timid." he roared. His eyes nearly glowed with excitement and near ecstasy as his mind swung dangerously to a craving for power.

As James watched Alan slammed his hands down on the pillars and then froze. A wash of power lashed out from the pillars and knocked him back nearly twenty feet. He rolled head over heels clutching the codex to his body as he tried to shield the fragile volume from damage. Then he scrambled to his feet and watched as the arcs of power jumped back and forth, each time they traveled through the headpiece and Dr Stewart's body he convulsed and cried out in pain.

The pulses seemed to go on forever until James assumed that Alan's life had been completely driven from his battered body. Each time the light flashed through the headdress it took a darker and more sinister look. Finally the flashes stopped and Alan's body slumped from the device and collapsed to the floor.

"Alan!" James shouted as he gathered the courage to rush forward. Gingerly he rolled Dr Stewart's body over and checked for a pulse. Amazingly he found it immediately and it was strong and steady despite the battering that he had received. Once he knew that Alan was still alive he wrapped his hands under Alan's arms pulled him away from the device.

"James..." Alan's voice spoke hoarsely like a person who is parched for water.

"It's alright, Alan. You are going to make it."

"Hahaha, make it... you fool. I am so much more now..."

James scrambled back as darkness filled Alan's eyes. It seemed that the darkness of the beam of light was alive inside Alan's body. As the words faded Alan slumped to the ground again and appeared to fall into a deep sleep.

"Alan?' James said. Carefully he approached the inert form and checked for a pulse again. It was still there and it still seemed strong but his face seemed pale and his skin was cold to the touch. "Looks like he is going into shock."

Unsure of what to do James wandered the chamber for almost an hour. He examined every corner and wall before giving up and returned to where the headdress waited for him. He stood before the device wondering what to do as the beams of light mesmerized him. The luminescent shafts still shone down brilliantly from above and James found himself drawn towards the headdress. Slowly he took the headpiece in his hands and turned it over to examine it. It appeared to be carved from the same metal as the pillars but it was covered in precious stones and metals. Along the inside of the skull cap there were golden nubs that stuck out from what was a perfectly smooth surface.

"Well, I suppose it doesn't appear to have killed Alan." James ran his hand across his scalp once to smooth his hair and slipped on the headdress. He found that it molded to his scalp but that the golden nubs dug into his skin making it somewhat uncomfortable. Cringing he stretched his left hand out and slid it into the indents on the left pillar but except for a tingling sensation that filled his arm nothing happened.

"Alright already!" He made his decision and raised his right hand. With a firm motion he slid his hand into the right pillar and then froze.

"Ahhhh..." James screamed. His mind exploded in a torrent of fire, he felt that every nerve in his mind and body was burning. On and on the agony washed over him in waves then as suddenly as it had begun the pain faded and was replaced with a feeling of intense longing and sadness.

* * * * *

Suddenly he found himself standing on a dirt path, before him the trail split leading off into the distance. To the right a wide path led to a massive mountain and the Mayan glyphs for power and control were painted in black on a stone marker before the trail. To the left was a narrow path that led out towards a wide plain. Before him a stone marker carved with the Mayan glyphs for mercy and then power.

"You should choose now!"

James jumped as a voice spoke from beside him; he turned and gaped at the man that stood beside him. He was dressed in Mayan garb and his skin was deeply tanned from constant exposure to the sun. He folded his arms and waited as James stared at him in confusion.

"What is this?" James asked when he finally found his voice.

"Choose now. Will you take the power to control and dominate others? Or will you choose to mercifully sacrifice yourself for the good of others."

"Wait, don't go." James erupted but the phantom figure faded from view and was gone.

Again he faced the two paths and looked at the stone markers, "Merciful use of power or the power to control others. Well I know what Alan probably decided on. At least if he was provided with the same choice."

He looked down the roads leading to the mountain and almost immediately a feeling of revulsion arose within his spirit that nearly made him throw up. Shaking his head he turned and stepped onto the path leading to the plain and peace settled across his mind and body. The moment he stepped onto the path his view of this other world faded and he felt his body falling.

*****

James felt his body falling away from the device and landing on the floor. The headdress rolled off his head and settled to the ground beside him, immediately a feeling of weariness such as he had never felt before came over him. Try as he might he could not pull his body away from the pillars.

Suddenly the ground under him shook and another earthquake wracked the land around them. The last vision that he had was that of the lights over him fading away and the darkness closing in around him. Then he closed his eyes and slept.

6 Time Passes

Time passed slowly as the two men slept, unknown to them the flow of the years in this underground chamber differed from everywhere else. Outside the temple the great river of time continued to flow while inside they were protected from its ravages. With each breath the weariness that had driven them to the ground passed and then their bodies began to undergo a transformation. Not a physical one of their outside appearance but an inner change. The energy that coursed through them had rewritten many of the synapses in their mind. As time passed their bodies began to absorb energy from the world around them dipping into an eternal pool of power that had long gone unused. They slept for nearly ten years before slowly beginning to wake.

* * * * *

Strange are the worlds contained within dreams and nothing was stranger then the dreams that plagued Dr Kaning. He found himself standing on the narrow road that he had seen in his mind when wearing the headdress.

Before him in the distance the plain stretched out as far as he could see, it was featureless and without any form. As he walked, the trail led him down a long slope until he finally arrived at the edge of the plain. When he finally stepped off the trail the misty figure appeared before him and held out his hand.

"Now begins your true journey," the figure said.

"What do you mean?" James asked. As he watched, the smoky outline solidified into the same man of Mayan ancestry. He wore a feathered headdress and a simple loin cloth, on his arms were two gold bands which clasped around each bicep.

"It is here in this world that your spirit will gain strength and learn to view the world as it was seen thousands of years ago. You must relearn much of what you believe to be true."

James stared at him in confusion as he tried to decide exactly what to believe and what his mind was making up.

"Understand something Dr Kaning, this world is every bit as real as the earth. If you die here your body will weaken and die, however, while you are here you will not feel the effects of age on earth."

"What is this place that it is outside of the rule of time?" James asked. He looked around in wonder at the landscape around him and pondered how such a thing could happen.

"We are not outside the power of time; no one is outside of that. However time passes differently here. We do not know why but those who live here know it is true."

"Are you from earth originally?" James queried. His mind struggled to make sense of what he was being told.

"Yes, I was born on earth over six thousand years ago. I was one of fifty-two men and women buried alive inside the temple so that our souls could act as guides here in this realm."

"I didn't see any bodies or tombs inside the temple," James muttered.

"Come with me," the man motioned. "Walk with me and I will explain what we are allowed to explain."

"What do you mean allowed?" James baulked at the idea. "Do you mean something or someone controls this place?"

"Well of course." the man laughed. "There is a power that created all of this for our benefit. Many societies believe in the concept of a single all powerful entity that made everything, is it so hard to believe?"

"I have never believed that. I don't quite accept the idea of evolution either but I refuse to believe that someday I will have to answer for my actions." James explained as they walked. "My wife was a staunch Baptist and she hounded me constantly into going to church but that was never something I was interested in doing." James stopped as he realized he was rambling.

"Well, despite what you believe there is a creator out there. This place was designed to allow human beings to make the best use of the world."

"But why would we need power such as this?" James insisted.

"There were times when human beings did not need the powers that have lain dormant in their minds for thousands of years. When the powers of technology began to take dominance, the power of magic faded into disuse. Now the time has come for the power of magic to begin to hold sway again. From what I can see, technology is fading away."

"But why, won't people simply begin to develop computers and technology again?" James insisted. He had a hard time believing that the inventive spirit of the human race could be subdued so quickly.

The man shook his head, "I do not believe that technology will ever again hold sway. The meteor shower has put in place a permanent force around the earth that will forever block all advanced technology."

James's mind raced as he struggled to process the influx of details about how the world was changing. Around him the plain shimmered and began to show a dense cloud of meteors in high orbits around the world. He assumed that something in the meteors was magnetic in order for it to interfere with things on the ground below. "Like a permanent electromagnetic pulse effect?" he asked finally. "Or a permanent sun spot that interferes with earth's magnetic fields."

His guided nodded, "However, my friend, this part of our journey is coming to an end. You will sleep for a long time and sometime in the future you will awaken." he waved off James's stammered protests. "You must understand the world is changing and so is humankind. You are going to be the first in a long line of guides."

"What of Alan?" muttered James as he slumped slowly to the ground?

"You will not remember much of our conversation for many years to come but Dr Stewart as chosen a different path. Humankind has always had a choice and Alan Stewart chose the path of darkness."

"But..."

"No, just listen. There are two choices given to all men. Will you serve good or evil. That is the gift given by God to the human race. There are other races that have no such choice, during the time of technology they were unknown on earth but now that the time of magic has come they will once again become powers to be reckoned with. Now you must sleep Dr Kaning, sleep and allow your body the time to adapt to the changes sweeping over it."

7 Like Magic

"Uhh," James groaned as he struggled through the cobwebs in his mind. Suddenly his eyes snapped open and he looked around him. The room was dark and almost absent-mindedly he wished he had some light. Surprise filled him when in response to his wish a small ball of light appeared over his shoulder and illuminated the cavern.

"What the..." James exclaimed as he stared at the small globe of white light. It was powerful enough to reveal the chamber fully but not so powerful that it blinded him. He scrambled back away from the light and was terrified to see that it followed him no matter what direction he turned.

"Go away." He finally sputtered at the ball of light, again in response to his command the globe winked out of existence. All around the room was plunged into darkness.

"James, is that you?" Alan sputtered groggily.

James breathed a sigh of relief as he heard Alan's voice. Blindly he felt around his pockets until he found the flashlight. With the flick of his finger he pushed the switch and was greeted with a feeble stream of light that shown for less than a second and then died.

"My flashlight is dead," James said. He put the metal tube back into his pocket and carefully stood to his feet. He reached out with his arms and felt around for anything to guide him but found nothing but open space.

"What happened to that light from a moment ago? I saw you sitting there with a light just above your shoulder?" questioned Alan.

"I don't know what that was. All I remember was thinking how nice it would be to have a light when I woke up. Suddenly there it was just like I imagined it would look."

Alan grunted.

James was about to pull out the flashlight again and try it once more when a red flame appeared less than twenty feet away. It hovered over Alan's shoulder casting long shadows on the walls and filling the room with a rich crimson light.

"Wow, you did it too." James scrambled to his feet and looked around. The headpiece lay where he had dropped it, but other than that, the room appeared exactly the way it had when they had fallen asleep. Suddenly he staggered as the memories of what had happened flooded back over him. He sat down again hard on the floor and groaned under his breath, his hands clutched his head.

"What's wrong?" Alan asked with a cold almost dead sounding voice. He glared down at the weakling sitting on the floor nearby and felt nothing but scorn and contempt for him.

"Nothing, I just remembered what happened last night," James replied.

"You better check your watch," Alan snarled. Without waiting to see if James would follow him he turned and began walking to where the tunnel led back to the surface.

James turned his wrist and held the timepiece up where he could read it. The crystal face was scratched from the impact with the stone floor and he was forced to raise the dial close to his face to read the numbers. Long mocked for not wearing a more water and shock resistant sports watch he was now glad. The dial indicating the month and year told him that it was October of twenty-twenty but then he noticed that the timepiece had stopped working.

"Well that is not possible," James muttered. In a louder voice he called after Alan as he scrambled to follow the light, "How long does a watch battery last under normal conditions?"

"How should I know," Alan grunted as he approached the exit tunnel. "Probably years without being replaced."

"We can't have been asleep for almost seven years. Our bodies would not have survived without food and water for that long."

Alan shrugged, "Obviously something is going on down here that we don't understand." With those words he turned and walked towards the distant shaft that would take them back up the spiral stairs leading up to the temple.

James looked around one last time and then hurried after the receding light not wanting to be left in complete darkness. When he finally caught up with Alan he glanced at him but he seemed caught up in his own thoughts so he held his silence. Both men walked in silence until they reached the well.

"Looks like it might be broken further up."

James nodded as he surveyed the broken stones piled at one point across the room from them. "At least the reflector is still in place." He pointed to the round stone that channeled the beams of light down from the temple over them.

Alan showed none of the nervousness that had plagued him on the trip down. His stride was firm and confident as he led the way back up the shaft of the well. At two points they were forced to make a leap across collapsed sections of tunnel and Alan hardily slowed to see if James would make the jump. When they arrived at the top both men were winded and they leaned against the circular stone.

James's legs trembled with the exertion of the climb and sweat dripped from his face. Seated on a stone step next to him Alan's face was pale as his body struggled to take in enough air to fill his lungs.

"What now?" James asked when they both regained enough energy to stand.

"I would say we go outside and look around. It may be that someone or something at least survived the devastation."

James's heart beat wildly in his chest as they climbed the stairs that led to the surface. Much of the tunnel was damaged but amazingly enough had somehow survived the shockwaves that traveled through the earth for them to crawl out. Large chunks of limestone lay on the steps under where they cracked loose from the walls and ceiling but thankfully the hard packed dirt had not collapsed. The limestone blocks that blocked the entrance was a different matter. When they arrived in the rectangle room that connected the Temple to the outside world the room was completely black.

"We need more light," Alan muttered.

"How are you making that light stay here?"

"Beats me, I just knew we needed light and I thought that a torch would be handy. I had a picture in my mind of a flame and suddenly it popped into view."

"Let me try," James said. He closed his eyes and focused his mind on a picture of a white light that looked like a light bulb but without the physical device.

"Kind of bright isn't it?" Alan grunted in irritation.

James opened his eyes and squinted at the burst of light that left his eyes covered with a huge black spot. "Sorry" In his mind he pictured the light smaller and in response it shrank until it lit the room with a warm bright glow.

"Shall we dig out?" asked Alan. He glared at the offending stones angrily as if getting ready to attack them.

"I don't know. Let me try something," replied James. He walked to the pile of rubble and stood before it with his hands outstretched. In his mind he pictured the door rebuilt and the rubble removed. He nearly fell over when the crushed stone began to move. Before him the rubble groaned and then flowed out from where it had fallen. The limestone blocks that blocked their path rose up into the air and fitted back into the slots. It was like watching something out of a movie happening right in front of his eyes.

"Amazing..."

When the door was completely reformed, James stumbled as the horded energy that he gained in the last hour left him. Thankfully a brilliant burst of sunshine bathed across them as they stood in wonderment of their new powers. His light flashed feebly for a moment and then vanished as his energy ebbed out.

"Magic," muttered Alan. "It's like having magic power."

"I wish I could argue with you but I am too tired," James said with a smile. "I feel like I have been run through an old fashion roller dryer."

"At least the sun is shining," Alan said. He stammered when the sun faded and a distant rumble filled the air. Maybe it was not safe? Maybe the meteors were still falling and then would have to flee once again for their lives.

James nodded as he tried to catch his balance. Finally he took a deep breath and stood wobbly to his feet. Together they stepped outside the temple entrance and looked around.

8 Unexpected Blessings

At first James was hard pressed to see anything different from their vantage point. Out in front of him vast swaths of devastation surrounded several massive desolate craters. As they climbed higher the view to the west was that of a vibrant jungle trying to recover from a number of massive impact craters. About a mile from the hill he saw a deep crater still surrounded by downed trees but with a thick covering of ferns growing inside. Here and there small trees sprouted through the jungle floor.

"I think we were asleep longer than six years," muttered James. "I think my watch battery died after six years." He shook the device again and held it up to his ear as though he would be able to hear something from the electronics.

"Could be," Alan agreed.

James turned and began climbing the hill so that they could look to the north. High above them, riding on the winds, a thick cloud blew across the sky. Within moments it covered the sun and robbed the area of warmth. Wearily he finished struggling up the slope and gaped in amazement as he stared. In the distance a massive volcano now raised it's head over the landscape. Rivers of boiling lava still flowed down the sides and disappeared into the jungles blocking their view. A few small fires still burned around the edges of the lava flows and trails of smoke drifted high into the sky.

"Well, that wasn't there before," James said. He jumped as a distant explosion sent a massive column of smoke and bits of lava flying out of the cone. The valley below them appeared to have survived and thrived in the intervening time. Everywhere they looked verdant jungles filled their view despite the smoking behemoth that threatened to burn everything in its path.

"I am hungry," James said suddenly. On a whim held out his hand and concentrated but nothing happened. In confusion he thought about what he had done when rebuilding the temple door. "Maybe I have to be specific." This time he pondered what to think about and finally his mind settled on something simple. Again he focused his face on his hand and this time a flash of light erupted after a moment.

Alan glanced away and let his eyes clear when he looked back James held a red apple.

"How did you do that? More importantly can we make more of them?"

"Beats me. I tried to just create food and that didn't work so I concentrated on actually making an apple and it worked."

Alan looked at the apple thoughtfully and then held out his own hand. As he stared at the empty space his eyes narrowed in concentration. Moments later he held an apple that dwarfed James's for size and redness but even as the piece of fruit appeared Alan felt the bit of power leaving his body. "Obviously the laws of physics still hold sway over this power. You can't create something out of nothing. It felt like a bit of my strength went into the creation of the apple."

"How does it taste?" asked James. He looked at this unnatural piece of fruit suspiciously despite the grumbling of his stomach.

Tentatively Alan raised the apple to his mouth and took a small bite; dribbles of juice ran down his chin.

"Well?"

"Tastes great," murmured Alan around a second mouthful. He ate greedily and chewed as quickly as he could.

As his stomach roared loudly demanding to be fed James realized how hungry he was so he raised the apple to his mouth and took a big bite. *Alan was right* thought James the apple tasted better than anything else he had ever eaten.

"Why are we sitting on the ground," said Alan suddenly. He closed his eyes and a moment later two chairs grew up from the ground giving them a place to sit. When he finished with the chairs he staggered weakly as the use of power leached away his strength. Under the small thrones the ground sank slightly as the stone of the earth was drawn up and molded into a new use.

They sat on the chairs making and eating food for much of the afternoon, watching the intermittent explosions of the distant volcano. Neither one seemed to grow full until they had eaten enough food for ten men. Laughter filled the air as they tried to outdo each other, roast chickens took shape, and dozens of pies filled the mountaintop around them as they searched their memories for anything odd that they had ever eaten.

"I feel a million times better now that I am full. It was like moving the stones for the temple door left me all dried out. Now I feel like I could make a dozen more," he said drowsily. With their stomachs full the sudden urge to sleep began to overtake him.

"I think we should get back inside and get some sleep," said James. When he got no answer he looked over and saw that Alan was already asleep where he sat, a half eaten donut in one hand and a thick slice of pecan pie in the other. Slowly the donut dropped from his hand and landed on the ground with a sloppy thud that left apple filling oozing onto the ground.

Lurching wildly James struggled to his feet and stumbled to where Alan slept. Drunkenly he managed to hoist the other man to his feet and drag him back down the slope to the temple. His mind remained sodden with the need for sleep until he collapsed at the bottom of the steps leading into the temple chamber. With the last of his strength he transformed two slabs of limestone in the floor into serviceable beds and dropped Alan onto one. Then he walked the five paces to where his bed waited and fell on top of it.

The snores of both men filled the chamber and outside the sun and moon came and went hundreds of times. Then thousands as the seasons passed and the earth struggled to return to a semblance of normalcy. As they slept a slight glow of power covered each of the men holding them in its grasp and keeping the effect of time at bay.

*****

Once again James found himself standing on the trail leading out to the massive plain. This time the lands around him seemed more alive, blades of grass were shoving through the grounds around the trails and on the distant plain he thought he saw small stands of trees taking shape. As he watched, a range of mountains shoved up through the level surface complete with snow-covered peaks and a roaring waterfall rumbling off a high cliff. It was a world in flux as landmasses took shape and filled it with a vast diversity of features.

"Amazing, isn't it?"

James jumped as his guide appeared at his side, "I was wondering if you would show up again. What is happening out there?"

"Well, for hundreds of years this place has had no one to serve and has sat waiting. Now that someone who can use the power has arrived the land is responding to our calls. Once again this land can be a place of peace and tranquility, a place where you or any other that you decide to share your secrets with will be able to find rest for your weary minds. Truly it will be a land flowing with milk and honey and inevitably there will come dark days when you and your helpers will need a place of safety to restore your strength."

James shaded his eyes as a brilliant springtime sun broke through the gray sky and chased away the dull clouds that filled the sky. Already the forests towered fifty feet into the air and carpets of flowers covered the meadows. Somewhere out of sight the thunder of a waterfall filled the air.

"However, as comforting as this place will be some day, there is something else that you must see for there is a second side to this place of peace, a side being created or at least guided by your friend."

"Dr Stewart is here?" exclaimed James. He looked around excitedly hoping to see some sign of Alan. "Where is he and can I speak to him?"

"No, you will not see Dr Stewart while the both of you are here. But you will see what is shaping his place of refuge. We will see what has come to rule his mind," the guide explained as he motioned to the dark path leading away from the tranquil forests that now dominated the mountain-strewn plain.

James stepped onto the dark path hesitantly as his mind and spirit cringing at the shadows that flitted around the edges of his vision. He stopped immediately and baulked at the idea of continuing in that place of darkness.

"Come, you must see what is happening."

James nodded and forced his body to place one foot in front of the next. The land around him was cloaked in darkness but the shadows seemed alive with unspeakable beings. Each time he turned his head to catch a view of the things in the darkness he found he was unable to see anything around him. Slowly a bit of light grew around them but rather than finding its source from the sun, the light came from the glow of three massive volcanoes in the distance. Glowing rivers of boiling lava lit the land with an eerie light that moved and flickered and made the surrounding lands seem to move with a mind of its own.

"This is Dr Stewart's vision of the world and something that will be within his power to create if he is not challenged. That is why there are two of you, it's a balance between good and evil. This is how the world is being offered its next choice between good and evil."

"What is moving out there on the mountain side?" James squinted at the distant peak. He thought he could see small beings about the glowing rivers in long lines.

"They are spirits dedicated to evil. Spirits that will take physical shape on earth once again. Come let us see what is taking place."

"What do you mean once again?" James demanded. "I have never seen anything like that on earth."

"Where do you think the legends of goblins, vampires, and giants came from?"

James was unable to answer so he followed along tentatively as his guide walked down the wide trail leading towards the distant fiery mountains. Puffs of smoke erupted from the ground after each step and James found himself struggling for breath against the whirlwinds of dust and ash that surrounded him. He coughed violently as a strong smell of sulfur filled his lungs and robbed his breath.

"What are they doing?" James muttered as they drew closer to the strange looking beings. Some were vaguely human in shape but with fanged teeth and hooked claws. Others were massive in size and crawled on the ground like huge feral animals twisted with evil.

"They are getting ready for war, we should stop." His guide motioned for him to halt over a hundred feet from the creatures. "If we move any closer they will sense us, and they can kill even in this realm."

Nodding James stopped and watched in fascination as the creatures rambled back and forth across the landscape. The smaller goblin looking creatures seemed to erupt from spots on the ground from areas that look like piles of fleshy garbage. Creatures that seemed like wolves but with red eyes, two heads, and bits of fire erupting from their mouths on both heads roamed across the landscape attacking other creatures around them. The two headed wolves reminded him of ancient drawings of the mythical beast guarding the entrance to Hades in the old stories. How much of those stories were grounded in some reality?

"As you can see many of them require no food to multiply in this land and when they are loosed on earth they will be fully armed and ready for war. While humanity is struggling to survive, your friend will slowly become aware that they are his to command and when he does he will use them. Indeed, there is one race that he has already released into the ground. Thankfully, it will be many years before they are ready to serve him, still the war has begun."

James shuddered as his guide described the future that awaited the survivors on earth. "How can we stop them?"

"You cannot, they will come to earth no matter what you do. However, none of these creatures is indestructible and all can be killed. Given the right tactics and bravery they can be contained into the areas they already control."

Slowly they backed away from the molten rivers. When they had put enough space between themselves and the creatures they turned and walked quietly back to the head of the trail.

"So most of them take their names from creatures of legend?"

"Some have been called many things over the centuries. Hundreds of years ago an evil man managed to release some of the blood hungry into the world and they were so named by the people who ran into them. During their last outbreak on earth they were called Dhampir's by the people of the Balkan peninsula."

"Dhampir's? Why is that?"

"Because they feed on blood and the bodies of those they kill."

James shuddered, he stood silently looking out at the two landscapes but suddenly he felt very tired. "I think I need to sleep again."

"Yes, you will sleep this time for a very long time. The world will change as will your bodies, not physically but your mind and body will change giving you control over the primal powers placed in the earth at its creation."

James nodded and finally slipped off into dreamless sleep.

9 Dec 15, 2085

James awoke with a start, his mind reeling as he tried to reconcile the rocky ceiling above him with the dream of his wood framed home in St Cloud. In his dream his wife was waving to him as he left for work, his son played happily on the porch and on the horizon behind them a fiery meteor raced towards earth. Sweat soaked his body as he struggled to stand and save his wife and son. Drunkenly he rose to his feet and struggled up the steps, outside the sun was just rising and the brilliant burst of light made him shade his eyes. The landscape around him had changed drastically. This time he noticed it quickly as his mind cleared. The jungle now reclaimed everything but the nearby slopes of the hill.

When he crested the summit he fell into the remains of his chair and looked to the north. The valley that before was sparsely covered with trees was filled now. The trees grew so dense and the undergrowth was so thick that he was unsure if he would be able to pass. The volcano that was active last time they awoke now sat silent and vast swaths of green covered most of the lower slopes. Only the last few hundred yards closest to the top was still strewn with rocks and there was no sign of the vegetation breaking through the devastation nearest the top.

As his mind began to clear he glanced at his watch, the dial on the face was dead and it refused to start working despite his best efforts then he remembered why. "I wonder how much time has passed this time." Forgetting the dead timepiece he slumped back in his chair and watched as the brilliant orb of the sun rose into the air. It was mid morning and he felt like a man who had just been born, everywhere he looked things seemed new. Around him the world more brilliant, the clouds more defined and the forests more vibrant.

"I wonder where Alan is." James asked himself. His foot tapped energetically on the base of the chair. For the first time since donning the headdress, he felt full of energy in a way he never thought possible. When he could contain his excitement no longer he stood and returned to the temple entrance. The stones surrounding the portal were now covered in green moss and creepers. A multitude of spider webs waved in the light breeze where they had been scattered across the dark entrance when he stumbled through earlier.

With the barest of thoughts he summoned a brilliant globe of light and positioned it over his right shoulder. Absently he removed his watch and held it until he entered the central chamber of the temple. Carefully he put the timepiece into one of the many alcoves carved into the nearby section of wall. After leaving his watch he turned and surveyed the temple. The bed where he dumped Alan still sat where he placed it. Spread out on top of the mattress was the form of Dr Stewart. Light snores issued from his mouth on a regular basis until James finally reached over and shook his arm.

"Alan! Wake up, I think we have slept longer then we wanted."

Dr Stewart came awake with a start and the same dazed stare that James felt earlier covered his face. He yanked his arm away and looked around in confusion.

"What?" he shouted. "What are you talking about?"

"We slept for a long time," replied James again patiently. "Long enough that the volcano has stopped erupting and the mountain has grown over with trees."

"Must have been years. But..." Alan stammered. "How can we be alive if we slept for years?"

"I don't know but we are. Remember the volcano across the valley?"

"Yah," Alan answered.

"The forest has already reclaimed much of the lower slopes."

"So we are talking about decades."

"I would say that fifty years would be a low estimate. From the look of the trees I would guess more than that."

"Fifty years!" Alan was aghast. Almost in irritation he turned his face away from the brilliant globe of light hovering over James's shoulder. Alan raised his hand and stared for a moment. In a burst of red light and brimstone, a ball of fire appeared over his outstretched hand and muted the brilliant white of James's light.

"That is better," muttered Alan.

"Come out and see. The jungle has grown in leaps and bounds. It will be nearly impassable for travelers."

James bounced on the balls of his feet excitedly as he moved back to the steps leading up to the entrance. Behind him Alan followed at a slower pace muttering under his breath.

Five minutes later found them both standing atop the temple mound and looking out across the magnificent jungle. Now James heard the calls of monkeys hidden in the leafy foliage and the rustle of bigger animals as they stalked their prey. The animals had survived the devastation and flourished in the absence of humans.

"Think anyone else survived the meteor shower?" Alan asked suddenly. The burst of life around them seemed to make him withdraw even more. Spitefully he stared up at the sun over head, "Sun is too bright." he muttered. A glow of power surrounded him and he was quickly clothed from head to toe in a long black robe. His hands seemed pale as he reached up and flipped a large airy hood over his head and brought his entire face into shadows. "That's better." he murmured.

It was then that James glanced down at his own pants and shirt and realized how ragged they had become. His sturdy work jeans were threadbare and the seams holding the collared shirt together were frayed almost to the point of falling apart.

"Gandalf," laughed James after thinking about who he wished to look like.

"What?"

"Gandalf, you know. Didn't you ever watch the Lord of the Rings movies?"

"No," muttered Alan. His growing irritation went unnoticed by James who immediately began expounding a rendition of the trilogy of movies. When Alan had listened to quite enough he waved his hand and shouted, "Just get on with it!"

"Oh, alright," replied James in a more subdued tone. He closed his eyes and concentrated bringing the picture of a long flowing white robe to his mind. He thought about adding the pointed white hat to the outfit but wavered, finally he add the same type hood as Alan had produced and then opened his eyes.

"I feel like each time I use this power I give a bit of my own strength. Almost like the power is coming out of me and draining me," James muttered suspiciously. He looked down at the robes as if they had betrayed him somehow.

"I felt it too. We will have to be careful not to expend all of our energy at once." Alan smiled at the dour expression painted across James's face, "Come on we have a new lease on life and we were gifted a power unheard of for thousands of years. This is the chance of a lifetime, the chance to rule over this small world." James's muttered response was lost on Alan but he ignored him.

They stood for a while eating and contemplating the surrounding forests until finally James spoke.

"We should at least explore around us, you know, to see if anyone else survived."

Alan nodded but kept silent.

"I was thinking that maybe you could explore north and I could swing south. It would probably be better since I speak Spanish better then you do."

Alan nodded giving his ascent to the plan, "Whatever." He waved his hand over his shoulder and continued to stare out across the greenery.

"How long should we go for?"

"We should probably stay at a little closer to the temple just in case we have to sleep again. The last time I almost collapsed on top of the hill. If I had slept up here for fifty years who knows what wild animals would have feasted on my flesh," Alan said his voice drawing out the syllables in an almost serpentine fashion.

"Well, how about one month. Thirty days to explore and see what is going on around us."

"Agreed."

James turned and looked to the south, in his mind he imagined what Central America should look like. A snaky connection between Mexico and Columbia and most likely now covered in thick jungles. Whatever cities had once existed, were now in all likely hood crumbled ruins and being reclaimed by the surrounding plant life.

"Well..." James said as he turned back to where Alan had been standing. He stammered to a halt. Alan was already half way across the valley. Rather than walking he was floating about ten feet over the treetops and speeding away faster than a horse could run.

"Well, I am glad he offered to share that discovery with me."

James turned back to the south and wondered how Alan had done that little trick. Wind, he thought so he reached out to the wind around him and tried to push his body up and away. Finally he gave up after covering himself with dirt and rocks but remaining firmly rooted to the ground. After thinking for a bit longer he began to walk as he turned the problem over in his mind.

"Balloons," laughed James as he entered the thick jungles. In his mind he pictured a dozen balloons on strings tied to his waist. Finally he shook his head and continued walking. The ground rose noticeably as he traveled out of the valley, when it finally leveled again he found that it thinned a bit and he was able to at least see the sky overhead. There was a good breeze blowing from the north and it rustled the leaves around him and even sent a bit of dust swirling into the air.

"What if I made myself lighter," mused James. He stopped and willed himself to be lighter; seconds later he felt the wind pick him up and begin to push him into the air. When James opened his eyes he almost lost his grip on what he now termed a magic spell in his mind.

Below him the ground dropped away covered in a forest of green, "Too light," he gasped as he willed himself to be heavier. It took a few tries to get the proper sense of weight that would keep him about fifty feet above the tree tops. Already he felt the horded power in his body very slowly leaching away. Rather than travel in the air for miles at a time he settled for rising above the tree tops every few hours and looking for any sign of civilization.

As he walked he began to realize how vulnerable he might seem to wild animals. To make himself less of a target he took a long branch from a tree and formed a serviceable staff. As he walked he worked with the staff, straightening it and adjusting it here and there until it suited him. By the end of the first day he had changed the staff until it was harder then steel and lighter than a feather.

He slept the first night in a shallow cave between two massive boulders. With a bit of practice he managed to form a barrier across entrance that would keep the wild animals out. The next morning came with the chatter of monkeys and the scream of a wildcat somewhere off to the east.

James rolled the blanket he had created the night before into a small bundle and then stuffed it into a pack he fashioned for himself. Once he was done packing his few belongings he exited the sheltered lea of the stones and continued south.

* * * * *

The next four days passed without incident, each time he popped himself over the trees he spun a complete circle checking for smoke and at times resorted to using the wind to travel quickly for miles. It was mid morning on the fifth day when he spotted a thin trail of smoke rising over the thinning jungles. Over the morning the jungles slowly turned to wide expanses of grass and to his surprise he thought he smelled salt in the air. With the prospect of finally speaking to someone besides Alan he dropped back to the ground and began to jog in the direction where he marked the trail of smoke. The final break from the jungle came more quickly then he thought it would and suddenly he found himself standing at the edge of a small village. Even more surprising was the sound of ocean waves breaking against the shore nearby.

James was still wearing his white robe when he left the confines of the jungle and the sudden burst of sunshine left him sweating almost immediately. He reached up and flipped his hood back as he surveyed the village. He found himself standing on a small rise looking down at the circle of thatched huts about twenty feet away. Even more startling was the looks of the small group of people huddled near a communal fire. Four men and five women stared up at him as a baby cried in the background.

Silence descended on the group except for the crackle of the cooking fire and the insistent cries of the child. Everyone stared with wide eyes as though they had seen a ghost. Finally James smiled and began walking down the slope towards them. The moment he moved the group scattered, bronzed bodies fled and long locks of black hair strung out behind the men and women. He stopped but it was too late, the village was empty except for the angry baby who continued to demand attention.

"Hola!" James called. His voice echoed shrilly in the empty space around the fire. He called out several more times hoping that the sound of his voice would draw the people back. This was not the way he envisioned meeting the first group of survivors that he met.

"Hola?"

James nearly danced for joy when a small voice answered him from the dark recesses of a nearby hut. Happily he turned and smiled as a small girl stepped from the darkness and looked up at him. She examined him for a moment and then walked to where the infant continued its cries. Cooing to the baby she picked it up even though she staggered under the burden.

"Thank god for the bravery of children," sighed James. He smiled again and sat down on a nearby log. Slowly he motioned the child closer as he reached into his pack and pulled out the first piece of fruit that his hand found. With a encouraging smile and nod he offered her an apple. She smiled and took the fruit. With a furtive glance at him she began eating in big bites.

"Are you a god?" she finally asked in rough Spanish. Expertly she seated herself on the ground near him and shifted the infant until it rested against her crossed legs. With that done she used both hands to furiously attack the apple until it had completely disappeared except for a small collection of seeds.

"Oh no, not a god. Just a man who has sought for other people for a long time."

She nodded and seemed to relax at his denial of godhood.

"Will the others return?" asked James. "I would like to speak with them." His desperation to speak with someone, anyone made his voice tremble.

"I will call them. They are not as brave as Maria. Maria knew you were not one of the bandito's." The little girl wiped her hands carefully on her rough spun tunic and smiled at him.

James frowned at the word. He knew the word well enough and he knew that bandits operating nearby meant trouble. He opened his mouth to ask another question but the little girl had already stood. Carefully she handed him the baby, turned, and scampered off into the forest. It must have taken Maria a while to convince the others to return because she was gone for what seemed like hours to James. The child in his arms was at first fussy at being near a stranger but finally gave up and nodded off to sleep. Her tiny nose flaring out each time she took a breath. Finally Maria returned with only two people in tow. In his arms the baby took that cue to awaken and let loose with a hearty roar.

James laughed to himself as he sat there rocking the infant, it cried for several minutes before suddenly stopping. It cooed up at him and smiled as he rocked it gently.

"Thank goodness you are back," James muttered as Maria approached he looked up at her and the others and smiled broadly.

10 Maria

"Who are you?"

James smiled at the blunt question, Maria had returned with a man and a woman. Both wore hand spun trousers, rough dirty short sleeves shirts, and wide sombrero type hats to keep the sun from their faces. Despite his smile both shifted nervously from foot to foot and their eyes darted about wildly refusing to meet his friendly smile.

"My name is Dr Kaning. I was exploring an ancient temple to the north when the sky burned..." His voice faded off as he noticed the blank look on both of their faces.

"Were you sent by the Dark Runners?"

"What are the Dark Runners?" asked James in confusion. Evidently the look on his face must have convinced them that he was speaking the truth because both of them relaxed visibly. He waited patiently hoping that an explanation would soon follow.

"They are a group of banditos. Their leader has pushed us from our homes to the east and kidnapped our people until only a few remain," the man explained.

James frowned at the news and his sense of indignation rose up at the exploitation of people by their fellow survivors.

At times like this, people should be banding together to survive instead of preying on each other.

"I have a question for you," James said. He raised his hand to stop the sudden flood of words that now came at such a pace that he was unable to keep up with the flow. The woman was gesturing wildly to the east and the man was slamming his fist into his left hand. Both of their faces were deeply tanned and weathered from constant exposure to sun and wind. He waited until both fell silent and then asked the question that had been bothering him since waking.

"How long has it been?" James asked in halting Spanish. He waited but both stared at him blankly, they were silent for such a long period of time that James thought he must have said something wrong.

"How long has it been since the sky fell," he tried again. He was unable to remember the word for meteor so he stammered out what he believed to be a close translation.

"Where are you from?" the man asked. He looked at him closely not sure whether he was insane or serious.

"Originally I was from Minnesota," James explained. More blank stares greeted his statement so he explained further. "It was a state in the United States."

"Ah los Estados Unidos, yes we have heard of that country. It has not been called that since before my mother was born," the woman replied. She stared at him in interest and in surprise. "Our legends say it was a powerful land with many wonderful things. But for all its power it was unable to do anything when the sky burned."

"But how many years?" pressed James. His hands shook and his heart pounded in his chest, a cold sweat dripped across his brow. To his elation she started counting on her fingers and scrunched up her face in concentration.

"I think it would be around ninety-seven years. Maybe ninety-eight." she smiled like someone who had just accomplished a great feat. Her smiled faded quickly at his reaction and a look of concern covered her face.

James sat down suddenly on the ground, his mind stunned at the revelation despite the fact that he tried to prepare himself mentally. Everyone he knew that might have survived the meteor shower would now be long dead to disease and old age. Survival meant nothing to the inevitable march of time outside of whatever affected the interior of the temple.

"Are you alright?" Maria ventured. With wide eyes she stared at him in concern.

"Yes, just surprised," James finished lamely. Carefully he handed the infant back to the woman with a last smile at the young life struggling to survive. Absently he reached back and took an apple from his pack and bit into the bright red fruit. Suddenly he noticed the stares directed at him so he reached back and took two more from pack and handed them to both adults.

"Oh, Gracias, senior."

James nodded at the woman and smiled. With the small gesture a feeling of happiness pierced the veil of blackness that threatened to overwhelm his spirit. When he finished the apple he tossed it down in the fire and wiped his hands on his robe. His mind remained so worried about his own problems that he missed the surprised look on all three faces when he causally tossed away the apple core.

"Sir, can you help us," Maria asked finally. The words came in a tumble as she kicked at the ground with her bare feet.

"With what?" James replied. His mind was still a thousand miles away as he pictured his wife and son. For some reason he could not reconcile himself to the fact that both were long gone and nothing he could do, would ever bring them back.

"The banditos will find us soon and will take away more of our people. We do not know how to fight them. It is said that the old Estados Unidos was a strong warlike nation. If anyone can help us you can," Maria said fiercely. Her face filled with naked aggression as she fiercely gestured to the east.

"But I am not a warrior," James said gently. "I was a teacher." His voice faded off as he watched their faces fall in disappointment. "But that being said, why don't you tell me about these banditos and I will see if I can do something."

Their faces brightened visibly and a moment later the man rushed off into the jungle. He called something about bringing in the rest of the village over his shoulder but his words were lost to the trees. The Spanish that they spoke was so different then what he remembered and it was hard to follow then when they spoke too quickly.

"Do you have any more apples Dr Kaning?" Maria asked slowly. A smile danced about the corners of her mouth as though she knew he would say yes.

"Hold on," James replied. Carefully he reached into his bag under the flap and began creating an apple each time he reached into the pack. In quick succession he made a dozen apples and brought them one at a time from his pack. Maria's eyes were wide with amazement as he pulled them one at a time from the seemingly to small bag.

"It is magic," Maria said. Happily she ran to a small hut and retrieved a basket woven of grass and small branches. Grinning like a girl who has just found a store of candy she stacked the apples in the basket and then laid them carefully inside the hut.

"Not magic just a skill I learned some time ago," James said quietly. He was beginning to realize how magical and powerful his new skills would seem to the vast majority of the survivors. Also the fact that he would seem all-powerful might work well in convincing the banditos to leave the village alone.

The sun was nearing the treetops on its way around the world when the villagers began to filter back into the circle of huts. At first they came slowly and looked almost like they were ready to bolt at the nearest sign of trouble. Thankfully Maria took the lead and began to pull people toward the fire all the while keeping a running dialog so fast that James struggled to keep up.

When all the villagers seemed to have returned Maria brought out the basket of apples and began to hand two of them to each person. When she realized that she was six short she came to stand before James with her small basket held ready.

"Alright Maria, here you are." James smiled as he quickly pulled six more apples from his pack. Many gasps of surprise followed the appearance of each shiny red apple.

All told there were nine women, six men, and three children gathered around the fire when the sun finally set. The men went about gathering up firewood and built up a roaring fire, as the weather grew colder with the onset of night. James listened as Javier introduced the villagers and then told the story of their flight from a large group of thugs.

"We had a village to the east, there is large plain near the coast with two streams flowing through it and ending in the ocean. There we planted corn, maize and vegetables. Many days ago we spotted a large group of men and a few women riding horses and pushing down from the north. At first we thought they were coming to trade and we were happy. We soon found differently when they rode into out village and began to take our food."

James shook his head as he listened, in his mind he could see a peaceful community ripped asunder by the greed of other survivors.

"So we fled leaving our homes and taking what we could carry. But not more than three days ago they found us and took many of our people back with them to be slaves."

"Why didn't they take everyone?" James asked as the story drew to a close.

"Those of us who remain were away in the forest seeking a way to pass further to the west. There are rumors of a large group of survivors living far to the west."

James nodded, "How many did they take?"

"Twenty-seven, including my daughter," Javier said. As he mentioned his daughter his eyes filled with tears and his head hung in shame. Several of the others patted him kindly on the back and whispering the names of their own missing loved ones.

"I will see what I can do tomorrow," James promised even though his mind told him that it was an impossible task.

He slept that night next to the fire despite the offers of a space in one of the many huts. The night sky above him filled with stars that looked down at him and gave witness to the sad state of the human race. Battered and beaten, the few who survived now turned on each other some like rabid dogs going for the kill.

The next morning came and found James hiking east behind the thin figure of Javier. Before leaving he had awakened early and created a large amount of food. He tried to create things that would last for days and give the remaining villagers something to sustain them. The effort had cost him some but his body seemed to be recovering well as he nibbled on fresh fruits and vegetables.

They walked along a trail that mirrored the edge of the ocean. Off to the right a shallow cliff fell away to the ocean surf and to the left a narrow strip of grass separated the salt water from the heavy jungles further north.

As they walked James began to realize where he was, "Does the land extend further south?" He kept looking south searching for any sign of the bridge to South America.

"No," Javier said as he shook his head. "I explored many days travel to the west and the land curves back to the north."

"That means that the meteors destroyed much of the land bridge between Mexico and South America." He peered to the south trying to see if he could make out any sign of land across the salt water but he could not.

"We found a map that survived the fire storms that filled many of the old cities. It is as you say, at one time our lands divided two great bodies of water. That is not so any more, something happened to the land that used to bridge across the ocean to the south and it sank below the water."

"Not by much though," James said as he studied the water. "Look, it is very shallow for miles out from the shore."

"But it is filled with sharks. The oceans have done well since the sky burned. Our village had several fishing boats and we never lacked for fish," Javier explained. He looked sadly at the water to the south and patted his stomach fondly.

They walked for most of the day and only camped when the scream of a jaguar echoed through the nearby trees. Javier led the way down to the beach and they slept on the sand in the shelter of a pile of driftwood. The next morning was cloudy and a drizzle of rain began soon after they awoke.

It was still raining when they arrived on a hill overlooking Javier's village. A wide plain spread out for nearly a mile before ending in a collection of timber huts and a couple of surviving brick and mortar buildings.

James examined the village from where they crouched behind a small bush but from the distance he could only see small bits of movement. He was too far away to begin to plan any type of rescue so he motioned to Javier.

"We need to get closer," James whispered. Carefully he slipped down the hill and entered the edge of a cornfield. The plants around him were chest high and he crouched down to avoid being seen.

"Dr Kaning look," Javier pointed when they reached the edge of the field. The walls of the first hut were less than twenty feet away. Two rough looking men with dark skin stood guard over a huddle group of miserable looking people.

"That is more than just your village isn't it?" James whispered. He counted quickly and stopped when he reached sixty-two.

"Yes amigo, many more. But I do not recognize many of them. Mother of Mercy!" Javier hissed suddenly.

James looked out and saw that two more men had appeared and were unchaining a pretty young woman from the group. She fought like a wildcat but was no match for them, soon she was dragged away from the group and tossed bodily into the nearby hut. Before she disappeared into the darkness she looked up and he almost thought she stared straight at him. Her hair and eyes were coal black and her skin was deeply tanned but without the weathered lines of years in the sun. The fear that filled her face could not disguise her beauty and James knew he had to rescue her.

The two guards laughed as one man took up a post outside the hut and the second one stood in the door leering into the darkness. Then with a rude gesture at his fellows he stepped into the hut and slipped a makeshift door shut.

"Hurry Dr Kaning, they are taking my daughter." Javier pleaded with tears filling his eyes.

"Come on, we need to get behind the hut," James wriggled across the field as fast as his arms and legs would push him. In seconds he reached the edge of the huts without being seen and jumped to his feet. In a moment of regret he glanced down at his robe and then hitched it up around his knees so he could run faster. When he reached the hut he gripped his staff tightly and used his power to rip away the layer of galvanized steel that covered the back wall. Standing inside staring at him was a dirty man in the process of undoing his pants and a young woman crouched in the corner.

"You have one chance to run," James said in a deadly voice. The thought of what was about to take place filled him with rage. Hastily the man before him slipped his tattered belt back into place and drew a rusty machete from a leather scabbard on his side. With a shout he raised the weapon and charged.

"Wrong choice," James growled. He raised his staff and pointed it at the man and willed an invisible fist of power to strike his attacker. The effect shocked even him it seemed a freight train slammed into the bandit. His body was physically lifted from the ground and sent backwards with enough force to take the door from its hinges and send half of the front wall exploding outwards. "Hmm, maybe that was a bit too much power." The bandit slammed to the ground outside the hut and lay deathly still.

Rather than waste his moment of surprise he walked through the shattered remains of the front door and watched as eight more bandits scrambled from their shelters. Further out near the shore nearly a dozen more were gathering mounts from a makeshift corral and they turned to look at the sudden explosion in confusion. James saw the surprise written across their faces.

"Kill him!"

James glanced up the hard packed dirt street to where a particularly tall and muscular man wielding an old cavalry saber shouted orders to his men. Before he could decide on stopping the leader, the eight bandits raced at him brandishing an assortment of rusted weapons.

In a flash of thought James sent a blast of power into the ground before the trio on the left, the force of the power made the ground explode in an eruption of dirt and rocks. The release of power was so great that all three men were tossed like rag dolls into the air nearly ten feet. He stumbled for a moment as a wave of weariness passed over him but his anger at the bandits was so great he shrugged off the loss of strength.

Everyone stopped and stared in amazement as the back draft of wind from the explosion made his robe billow wildly and nearly knocked him off his feet. With a shout the middle trio charged forward brandishing their weapons while the pair on the right glanced at their partners nervously. In his right hand James held a handful of small stones and he threw them in a wide arc. A quick burst of energy made half of the pebbles explode in small explosions of light and smoke. The blasts blinded the men and sent them rolling on the ground as they clutched at ripped faces and blinded eyes. He was sweating now and he prayed he had the energy to finish what he began.

"Fire!" James cried. Immediately a wide arc of flame erupted from the ground and forced the remaining thieves to a halt. In the scramble to get away from the explosions and flames one of the men slipped on the dirt and rolled directly into the fire. James nearly let the flames go out as the screams of agony erupted from the thug on the ground.

"Go now, or face my wrath!" he cried. With his naturally deep voice he needed just a little bit of power to amplify his voice so that is echoed off the blacked clay walls. The remaining men took one look at him and threw down their weapons, the last James saw of them they were fleeing to the north into the jungles.

They would not stop running for a long time and he doubted that they would return to this place ever again.

Matthew J Krengel

11 One Kiss

"Holy Mother!" Javier muttered as he slipped by James and hurried to where dozens of frightened faces stared at him. In the heat of the moment he forgot that not only the raiders were watching him, but so were the captive townspeople. The town's folk had seen what he could do and the fear in the air was palatable.

Many were crossing themselves and muttered under their breath, James heard the whisper of 'el Diablo' from several sets of lips. Again this was not what he wanted people to think when they saw him.

Deciding that the time for theatrics had come and gone, he reached up and removed his hood. He saw a visible sigh of relief when the chained people were able to see his face and knew that he was a man too.

"Amigo, can you help me get the chains off?"

James nodded, thankful for the distraction but the small gesture made his vision swim as the intense use of his power took its toll. When he thought he could walk without falling James hurried forward and pushed his sleeves up. Rather than employ his power to remove the chains and risk collapse, he picked up a rusted hammer dropped by one of the raiders and knelt down by the first villager. The chain was thin and in poor shape but it still had enough strength to resist tearing apart easily. Each of the captives had a circle of iron around their ankles, each of the iron shackles had an eyehole where the chain passed through and held the shackle closed.

"Hold still," James said. Carefully he lined up the chain on a stone sticking out of the ground and then brought the hammer down hard on a single link. Four blows later the chain separated under the blows and the grateful people set to work passing the chain down the line and feeding it through the locking mechanisms.

There were five separate chains to be broken off and the sun had returned after driving off the rain clouds. Overhead the fiery orb was beginning to set when everyone was finally free.

"What will happen now?"

Javier smiled at him, "We will be able to return to our village here. Even more we have invited some of the others to merge with us and found a city here. There is plenty of fresh water and more than enough housing and farmland."

James let out a hearty shout and shook Javier's hand vigorously. All around them the mummer of a dozen conversations filled the air as the villagers mingled and celebrated their freedom. The sight of those survivors coming together made his heart soar.

"What if the raiders return?" James asked finally when he was able to get Javier alone. They stood in the central building of the village. From the layout of the walls and surviving bits of roof, James thought it might have been a school at one time. Three long halls stretched out in a horseshoe and nearly a dozen smaller room connected to each hall.

"We do not know," Javier shrugged. "It was suggested that we learn to fight but we have no teacher for such things. Some asked if you would stay." The rise at the end of the statement told James it was a question and he was careful to hold his face neutral.

"I wish I could my friend," James said finally. He paused as Teresa appeared in the nearby door and looked questioningly at her father. There was a fire burning in the central square and the flickering of the nearby flames made her golden skin shine in the light. Suddenly he was acutely aware that it had been many years since he had talked to people let alone seen a woman as beautiful as Teresa.

"I have many things to do yet before I return to..." James trailed off unsure of how much to reveal. It was not that he did not trust Javier but with the lengthy isolation at the Temple he felt that discretion was better than freely offering the knowledge.

Javier fell silent as he sensed James's discomfort; instead he smiled and led James out of the shadowy hall and into the wide circle of light. As the moon rose into the night, the sounds of singing and laughing filled the schoolyard. James found that after the initial fear the people of the village were friendly. Many smaller cooking fires were lit and soon the smell of oil and roasting meat filled the air. The food consisted of raw vegetables, fresh oranges, ripe bananas and meat filled pastry.

As the night wore on James found himself dancing wide circles around the fire with the laughing villagers. Javier looked on smiling as Teresa cornered him and swung about as they threaded through the dancing crowd.

"I must get some sleep," James said finally. The moon had peaked and was beginning to dip in the sky. Overhead the stars shown more brightly then he had ever seen before.

He was exhausted and almost falling over as he tried to fend off the calls to dance.

"We have arranged a place for you to sleep," Javier said as he stifled a tremendous yawn.

The next day James slept late and when he finally rolled out of bed he found that Maria and the rest of the villagers had arrived and were in the middle of a joyous reunion with their relatives. Despite the early hour the impromptu party of the night before was repeated that day and into the evening. This time James went to sleep earlier and rose as the sun did the next morning.

While the rest of the people slumbered he prowled the old school, opening doors rusted shut for decades. All told he found a small library, a kitchen area, the principal's office, and concrete stairs leading down to the boiler room. To his surprise the boiler was well preserved but lacked oil for fuel, however the downstairs room was cool and well protected. In the library, most of the books had long ago been destroyed and only a few remained. Carefully he removed a volume from a dark corner of the bookshelf and laid it on a windowsill. With the light of the rising sun he read the faded script on the cover.

"Interesting," he muttered. The book was a pictorial recording of ancient Mayan culture. The pages were aged and faded but surprisingly the spine of the volume was in good enough shape to keep it from falling apart. As he paged through the book James continued to run over in his mind the situation of the villagers around him.

When he reached the end of the book he carefully returned it to the shelf and walked to the door. Instead of returning to his small sleeping area he walked to the downstairs boiler room.

When he was by himself he pulled a rusted piece of pipe from the wall and examined it. The ancient Mayans had not used steel in their weapons but he decided to try his hand at making weapons anyway.

With the door at the top of the steps closed he began his work. At first he lengthened the bar until it was about three feet long. When he was satisfied with the length he formed a crosspiece and fastened it to the end that he decided would be the hilt. It did not take long to make a comfortable handle but the blade took a bit longer. About thirty minutes later the weapon was complete and he set out about hardening the steel until he was sure it would never rust or need sharpening.

He stayed in the boiler room for the rest of the day experimenting, he found that if he tried beginning with stone it was nearly impossible to transfigure it to steel and make a serviceable weapon. He also found that the closer the base metal was to the size he needed to faster he was able to make the weapons. That night he had completed twenty swords and formed racks into the stone walls to hold them.

When he emerged from the boiler room he found it was dark already and the smell of food nearly made him wild with hunger. Using the power definitely made him hungry and he went in search of food.

He slept for nearly two days in a state that was nearly a coma; later on the third day when Javier woke him he lay groggily in bed for nearly two hours before trying to stand.

"Are you alright my friend?" Javier asked. Worry filled his face as he rubbed his hand across his forehead. "You are not sick are you?"

"Yes, I was working on a special project and it took much of the energy that I gained over the last few days."

Javier stared at him curiously for a moment but then shook his head, "I think I am better off not knowing."

"I will tell you when I am ready," James assured him. He waited one more day and then returned to the boiler room. A survey of the room told him that it was undisturbed. This time he carried a large bundle of sticks under his arm and he set those along the furthest wall. Choosing one that was nearly as tall as he was he straightened the rod and filled in the creases and cracks. When he held a perfectly round staff in his hand he hardened it until he was sure it would withstand even the hardest blows and then set it in another rack made for the staves.

The entire process with the staves took much of the morning but he found that working with wood was much easier then working with steel and iron. When there were thirty poles in the corner all nearly seven foot long he took thirty stones and in quick fashion made thirty spear tips and then went about fastening them to the poles.

The entire process took him up to almost suppertime and the sun was riding low in the sky when he emerged from his dungeon. This time he took his food with him and went in search of Javier, it was time to share his secret.

"Ah, there you are my friend." Javier walked down the village road towards him with a curious look on his face. "So this is where you have been hiding for the last few days."

They were standing in front of the old school and James motioned behind him. "Come with me."

"Alright," Javier replied.

James nodded, "I must leave soon but I wanted to make sure you were in a position to defend yourself if needed." Rather than wait until he had completed his project, he held the door open for Javier and followed him down into the boiler room. The room looked completely different then the first time he walked into it. The pipes that covered the walls were gone and sturdy racks covered two walls each filled with shining swords and dark wooden spears.

"My friend..." Javier's voice faded as he looked at the arsenal. With shaking hands he brushed away the tears from his eyes and wrapped James in a heartfelt hug.

"I will be finished in two more days, and then I will rest for a day before leaving. There are still a few days left before I must return to ..." James stopped as he struggled again not sure what to reveal to Javier. He had no wish to see a world where mad men gained the abilities that were developing within him. Rather than finish, he led the way back out of the armory and walked slowly to where the cooking fires were being stoked. "Well, where I came from, I have a friend to meet there."

When he was done eating James walked to the old library and continued his search for books that might have survived. The small orb of light hovered over his shoulder for hours as he carefully checked each shelf and storage drawer. Some of the metal cabinets were rusted shut from disuse and he was forced to employ magic to open them. Slowly the cabinet doors slid open revealing the inside of the first one.

"How do you do that?"

James jumped at the voice. Knowing whom he would see he turned and smiled at Teresa who stared at him from the door. She gazed at the hovering ball of light with a mixture of curiosity and fright.

"You must be a god to do such a thing."

"No, I'm not a god, just a man who has outlived his time," James muttered. Finally he sat down on the floor and motioned for her to sit by him. Three books he managed to salvage were arranged on the floor before them so that he could read the titles.

One was a science textbook but the other two were children's books.

"What do your people remember of the events from a hundred years ago?" James asked. Under the stare of her jet black eyes he shifted nervously as he suddenly became acutely aware of how close she was. She smelled of the beach and the sand still clung to her feet and legs.

"The days when the sky fell. My father says God grew angry at the way men acted. Papa says He took away his faithful and then he sent seven angels to cleanse the earth." Teresa shifted a bit but her stare remained locked on James. "I think that much is true, God sent his angels to cleanse the earth. Those of us who survive now must learn once again how to live and see if we can do it better this time."

James nodded, "My colleague and I were archeologists searching for a site north of here. We were caught by Hurricane Erik and then trapped underground by the meteors that fell from the sky. Whether this was God's doing or an act of nature I am not sure. All I know is that the people who lived here many years ago foretold what would happen. They built a place of security, of sanctuary; we were lucky enough to find it and it changed us. Now we are trying to find out how many people of the human race have survived..."

James trailed off as Teresa leaned close to him and lightly brushed her lips against his.

"I never thanked you for saving me," she whispered

"What would your father say," James heard his voice whisper.

"What I do is none of my father's business. If you are leaving soon then I wanted to at least give you a kiss, something to say thank you and for you to remember me."

Again she pressed her lips to his and this time with much more force. After the lingering kiss faded she stood and left the room with her head bowed sadly. It was if she knew she would never see him again

12 Goodbye

James woke with a start the next day. He struggled to stand as he untwisted his robe from around his legs. The books still lay on the floor where he had set them the night before. Teresa was nowhere to be seen and he felt oddly sad as picked up the books and placed them back on the shelf.

After eating a light breakfast of fruit and vegetables he returned to the boiler room and finished his work there. When he was done he looked around one last time. The boiler was gone, in its place were thirty steel swords, and thirty matching shields made of wood but bound with steel straps. Thirty spears and thirty bows leaned against the far wall each with a quiver of arrows next to it.

Sadly he walked down the empty hall of the old school and stepped out into the central courtyard. Javier spotted him from across the village square and waved happily to him. James returned the wave and absently began searching for Teresa, hoping that he would be able to say goodbye to her.

"Hello amigo," Javier smiled. He lay down the rough hoe that he was using and motioned to the nearby fire. "Would you like some bread?"

"Thank you," James broke off a hunk of the loaf and wolfed it down realizing for the first time how hungry he was.

"I am leaving in the morning."

Javier nodded sadly, "We will be sad to see you go."

"The armory is ready, I have supplied the weapons but it is up to you to learn how to use them. That is something that I have no knowledge of."

Javier nodded.

An awkward silence descended and finally James left and made his way back to the small pallet where his pack and blanket waited him. He lay there for almost an hour before sleep took and he dreamed a dark dream that left him shuddering in the half-light of the next morning.

13 Return to the Temple

James left village before anyone else rose that morning, he paused as he crested the nearby hill and looked back one last time. Teresa stood in the middle of the village watching him, he smiled and turned but she frowned at him and turned away. Confused and a bit hurt he almost stumbled to a halt and reversed course, then he nodded in her direction and hurried off to the north. In the back of his mind he knew that he would never see here again, his course lay in a different direction. She knew this and her refusal to even acknowledge him was her way of telling him it was better for him to simply keep moving.

The return trip to the temple took him nearly six days and when he finally spotted the hilltop he was searching for, the moon was full in the sky. He was floating fifty feet above the jungle staring down at the mass of trees and vines that covered the ground with a verdant blanket.

"There is it," James muttered under his breath. Carefully he slipped down to the ground and began hiking towards the distant hill. He estimated that he was only about a half a mile from the temple but it still took him nearly two hours of sweating and struggling through solid walls of plants until he broke through to the clearing around the temple. Atop the hill, near the two thrones, stood a dark figure waiting with a bit of flame burning over his left shoulder.

"Alan!" James called, behind him a jaguar screamed into the night and a sudden thrashing erupted making James hurry up the side of the hill.

"What took you so long?" Alan demanded. Angrily he stared down at James, his face locked into a grimace of hatred.

"Well, I found a group of people," James replied happily. In his excitement about finding survivors he missed the sudden gleam in Alan's eyes when he mentioned survivors. "I walked south for a few days stopping now and then to pop up over the tree tops and look for smoke. I assumed that anyone who would survive would have lit a cooking fire or two. Well I finally spotted a trail of smoke to the south and then found a small village of about twenty people."

"Bah, only twenty?" Alan growled. With a harrumph he threw himself down in the nearby stone chair and waved his hand for James to continue. "Hardly anything for us to use."

"Well they had just been raided by another group of survivors and over half of their people taken captive. There was a little girl named Maria who was brave enough to stay and talk to me. She managed to bring the rest of the people back, so then I went to their main village and managed to scare away the raiders."

"Where did the raiders go?" Alan said suddenly. Again the gleam returned to his eyes.

"I don't know," said James in irritation. "Probably ran off into the jungle and got eaten by wild animals. The point is that those people are now safe. I left them well equipped to defend themselves and there was even talk of other survivors coming to their town and joining them for mutual protection."

"Great," muttered Alan.

"There is another odd thing, before I left I got a bird's eye view of the land to the south. I think the impacts of the meteors cut the land bridge between here and South America. There was nothing but shallow water south of Javier's village. Probably, it is the remains of the Caribbean Ocean only now it is connected to the Pacific Ocean."

"I would image that there have been many changes to the shore lines around the world," Alan said absently. After the mention of finding survivors he seemed extremely interested but now he just appeared unconcerned.

"So what did you find?" James asked. He slipped into the chair next to Alan and stared up at the sky. Absently he slapped a mosquito that landed on his arm.

"You can keep those away from you, you know. If you visualize a barrier around yourself it will keep almost anything from hitting you. Just make sure to set in it an area for air to get it." Alan picked up a handful of dirt and dropped it against his robe. Just before the dirt struck him it stopped and slipped off an invisible barrier to the ground.

"Nifty," James said. Frowning he concentrated on the image of himself surrounded by a thin barrier but he left a small hole near his mouth. It did not take long to find out if it worked, a second wave of mosquito's arrived and despite their best efforts, none was able to land on him. Nearly a dozen landed on his arms and tried to bite his flesh and each left hungry.

"So what shall we do now," Alan said. His voice sounded tired almost like a man ready to sleep once again.

"I am tired, I am going down into the temple and go to sleep. I only hope that this time I am not going to sleep for decades," James said as he stood and turned towards the entrance to the temple.

"Why is that? Did you meet some girl?" Alan asked slyly.

"Well, there was a very beautiful woman there, her name was Teresa. She is Javier's daughter but I think she sensed that our relationship could not work out. When I looked back at the village she turned her back and walked away," James said sadly.

Alan snorted as they walked through the entry room, the stairs were pitch black and James released his hold on the shield. Instead he set his small light glowing merrily over his shoulder and when they arrived he stood staring at his bed. Despite his exhaustion he did not just collapse into the old mattress, first he knelt at the side of it and worked over the bed for a few minutes. When he was done a brand new looking mattress lay where the old one had been moments before. Finally he lay down and drifted off to sleep.

* * * * *

This time James knew what to expect and he waited patiently at the head of the trail leading down into the massive plain. As he waited he examined the areas that he could see from his high perch. Vast tracks of lands covered with thick verdant forests, flights of birds erupted from the trees and winged their way across the open skies. A small mountain range thrust up on the far side of the lands and it blocked his view of anything further out. Wispy clouds raced across the sky and out of the mountains tumbled a silvery band of water.

James looked out towards the other trail but he immediately shuddered and looked away. Feelings of dread and fear filled his mind and when he looked over, he caught a quick glimpse of the volcanoes and he thought that he saw the slopes crawling with all sorts of dark creatures.

"All is ready."

He jumped as his guide spoke from next to him, either the man was invisible sometimes or he could walk more silently than anyone else he had ever seen. But then it could be that the rules of physics were not the same here as they were on earth.

"Beautiful, isn't it?" his guide queried. He motioned out over the varied landscape before them and waved his arm to take it all in.

James took a deep breath as they began walking down the path leading to the lush plain. "Yes it is, but what is it all for?" They left the trail finally and walked across a sunny meadow filled with flowers. Bursts of red, purple, and yellow greeted him on all sides while a babbling brook flowed out of the forest on his left and disappeared into a thick stand of weeping willows.

"This is our place of rest, a place where as your body sleeps your mind can still learn and grow. As your physical body restores itself on the material plane your mind can restore itself on this plane."

"Will I be sleeping for extended periods of time?"

"Not nearly as often but yes there will be times when you must sleep for years."

"But why?" James pressed. "Is there something negative that using the power does to me?"

"Can you run a race and not be tired? Can you work for days on end and not rest?" his guide asked. "No one can. Yes, your bodies and minds now can access and control the vast pool of power that people commonly refer to as magic.

However, the more power you use the more rest you will require and the more often you will have to rest."

"And when I am resting on earth my mind will be here learning and resting?"

"Yes, you can build a place of refuge here and when you do finally die on earth. Your spirit will be sent here to help those who come after you learn just as I have spent centuries waiting for the chance to pass my knowledge."

James walked for many minutes in silence, they crossed the meadow after leaping across the brook. The forest on the far side was filled with life and it seemed that each shadow held the furtive shape of foxes, squirrels, and myriads of other creatures.

"Are all the animals here the same as on earth?" James asked finally. Before him two white tailed deer looked up from a patch of clover and then bounded into the forest.

"This place is a reflection of life on earth, but there are differences between here and the mortal world. First off, on this world it is not completely safe, there are times when the creatures of this world can and will threaten you. However, if you are paying attention to your surroundings you should be safe."

James nodded, not completely understanding but knowing that there were some things that he would probably have to figure out for himself.

"That is why I tell you to choose a place in this world and establish yourself a place of refuge. Many of the physical properties of this world are the same as on earth, wood is still a building material, stone is still hard, and water will still quench your thirst."

"I understand. So I should find a place that fits my personality and then create a fortress of solitude in so many words."

"Yes, there is one other thing. James you are the first in many thousands of years to come to this world. Those who came before you grew tired of waiting for others to come and made that final voyage beyond the furthest horizon. They can never return, I alone waited for the next master wizard to arrive. Now that you are here I will be making my final journey."

James protested almost immediately, "But how will I know what to do? This is so new to me how can I be sure I am making the right decisions?"

"Follow your heart. That is the best advice I can give. Also beware your opposite, he too will establish a fortress of his own. And he will work tirelessly to dominate the world."

He nodded as his guide finished speaking.

"Goodbye, James Kaning and good luck."

Without another word his guide turned and walked away into the forest. It seemed that he was heading towards the mountain range, James watched until he was out of sight and then he leaned against a nearby tree and pondered his next step.

"Well, I have always enjoyed mountains so I think I will find a place near the mountains to build my home here." No one answered him so he stood and walked toward the mountains. He walked for the rest of the day and as night fell he slept on the leeward side of a fallen tree. The next morning he rose early and continued in the same direction. As he walked he plucked fresh berries from heavily laden bushes and popped them into his mouth. Blueberries the size of his thumb and filled with juice stained his fingers and wild strawberries stained his robes with their crimson colors.

When he emerged from the forest he found that he stood atop the lip of a deep canyon, far below him a river filled the canyon floor and roared along under the frown of the nearby peaks. Rocky cliffs dominated the far side of the river but the sight that drew his eye was just upriver of where he stood. The canyon widened considerable upriver and it flowed from two sources. Where the rivers came together a rocky promontory jutted out over the rivers and gave a dominating view of the surrounding countryside.

"That is it, that is going to be my base." James smiled widely as he envisioned the soaring castle that he envisioned in his mind.

"That is a good place."

James jumped as a voice spoke from next to him, he whirled around and found himself looking face to face with a light green skinned humanoid. The figure was a woman and she stood to about his shoulder. Her hair was down nearly to her waist and it was a dark green almost black. What even startled him more was the fact that she was wearing a dress of what appeared to be leaves sewn together and wrapped around her body.

"I... ahh..." James stammered. It had been so long since he had talked to anyone besides his brief exchanges with Alan that he found his social skills wanting.

"Do you want help building your place of rest? There are many here who would willingly help you."

"Who are you?"

"We have always been here. It is our responsibility to help those who come here. If you must have a name to call me I have always like Rose."

"Uhh not to be rude but why is your skin green?"

"Because I live in a tree silly, I am tied to the plants and trees," Rose said with a matter of fact tone. "Do you need wood for your castle?"

"What makes you think I am going to build a castle?"

"Because that is what all of the mortals want when they arrive here. I don't know why but for some reason all of you humans seem to find it necessary to build a castle." She smiled to herself as if the thought of someone wanting to build a castle was the most amusing thing in the world.

"Has anyone else chosen this spot to build on?"

"No, I don't recall anyone ever choosing the stone outcropping as the sight for their home." Rose shifted her weight and stared at the triangle of granite and stone as though it was her most hated enemy.

James kept sneaking looks at her from the corner of his eye until he could finally take it no longer. "Are you an angel?" he asked.

14 The Spirit Realm

Rose laughed loudly at James, her long green hair shook wildly as she doubled up and laughed. "No I am not an angel, would to the maker that I was. They are a created being unlike anything else."

"Then what are you?"

"I told you, I am the spirit that represents the plants and trees of the world and more importantly this world. When the world was created my kind and I were created to watch over the flora, all that grows with roots in the earth is in our sphere of influence. Maybe years ago on earth we would have been referred to as a sprite, a spirit or a fairy."

"I don't believe in fairies and spirits," James stammered stubbornly. He folded his arms and pointedly looked away from her, sadly the image of her standing beside him soon had his eyes wandering back to where she stood. When he did finally manage to meet her eye he saw a flash of irritation that left him worried.

"Why I...," Rose stammered. "Well if that doesn't... That's it," Rose said. She turned away and walked to a massive oak tree and to James's surprise she stepped directly into the trunk and disappeared.

"Wonder where she went," James muttered as he stared at the brown tree trunk. Now that Rose was gone he found he missed her immensely and not just because she was beautiful but it was nice to actually have someone to talk too.

"I am mad at you," said Rose suddenly, her face emerged for a moment from the bark just above him. "I mean, do I look at you and tell you that you don't exist. The very nerve, he insults me after he spent most of the time staring at legs. Well that's it; next time I go out there I am going to drop a branch on his head."

James stepped back quickly as her face disappeared into the oak again and the thick branches nearest the ground began to shake violently. With a yelp of terror he scrabbled away until he thought he was clear of the reach of the branches. Suddenly a small branch swung violently out and arched out into the air. He watched in stunned surprise as branch arched towards him and then smacked him across the head. He stood for a moment stunned and then crumpled to the ground as the blow stunned him and robbed him of his senses.

"Oh, James I am so sorry," Rose whispered.

James wished the person groaning would stop and he raised a hand to rub his eyes trying to clear the cobwebs from his mind. Overhead the sun faded again as someone leaned over him and called his name. Suddenly the world snapped back into view around him and he was acutely aware that his head was resting in Rose's lap. Her soft hands slipped through his hair massaging the thick knot that throbbed in his skull just under the skin. It was then that the image of the branch flying through the air returned to him and he sat up suddenly.

"You hit me with a branch," James said accusingly.

"Well, yes, but I didn't mean it," Rose stammered. "We... I meant it at the time but..." Suddenly she broke down and giant tears began rolling down her cheeks. "I am so sorry. Don't tell any of the other spirits. They will never let me do anything ever again."

"It's all right," James muttered. He ran his fingers over lump and realized that it wasn't nearly as big as it felt. Beside the sight of the poor spirit creature shuddering under the wracking sobs was more then he could stand.

She sniffled loudly as the tears faded and held her arms out to him, "Please hold me."

James brightened visibly as he wrapped his arms carefully around her and stroked the back of her long hair. Suddenly he was fully aware of just out real the spirit world could be for him. Her skin was warm and soft and her hair smelled of spring flowers. Finally when he could stand it no more he carefully untangled his arms from around her and stepped back.

"Well, now that we are done with our first fight," James stammered. He turned away and stared at the outcropping of rock trying to clear his mind. "How do I get over there?"

"Well I am sure Gran could help with that. He could probably make a bridge," Rose said. She walked up to where he stood and leaned her head against his shoulder.

"Who is Gran?"

"Oh, he is so stuffy, it's always the ground needs this and the rocks need that. I mean they're just a bunch of rocks; it's not like if you stomp on the ground the rocks care. Now a tree, they can feel it if you hit them and they can talk if anyone cares to listen."

"Now that is something I did not know," James said. Again he carefully removed her fingers and hands from his arm and stepped away. "Do you think you can go get Gran and see if he will make us a bridge?"

"Oh fine but I warn you he is very boring." Rose turned and slipped into the tree leaving James to clear his thoughts.

"Goodness, trapped in a dream that is not a dream. With a tree spirit that has no idea of personal space. Not that I mind being close to her but I don't even know if things like that work in this realm."

"Who are you talking to?"

James jumped at Rose's voice directly behind him.

"If what things work in this realm?" Rose asked with childlike curiosity.

"Never mind," James muttered, unsure if she was teasing him or not.

"Rose, what is going on?" a deep voice asked.

James jumped as the voice echoed from directly below his feet. He was even more surprised when a face formed in a nearby boulder.

"Who is this?"

'This is James and don't try to hug him he doesn't seem to like it," Rose murmured. She sat down under the spreading leaves of the old oak tree and wrapped her arms around her bare legs waiting for James to speak.

"I was told that you can make a bridge to that outcropping of stone over there," James stated. He turned and looked at the face in the boulder and waited for a response.

"I can if that is what you wish. Are you certain that is where you wish for your castle to be?"

"Why does everyone here assume that I am building a castle?" James asked again.

"That is what your kind always builds," Gran replied with a straight face. "When Merlin came here he wanted a castle with four towers and a mighty gate. Then there was

Rasputin who wanted a castle where the snow never leaves the mountains."

"Wait a minute," James interrupted. "Those stories were true? But..." he sputtered. Those men were not that ancient."

"There were a few that came between the great deluge and now. But none in recent history."

"You mean there was really a great flood?"

"Well of course," Gran replied stately.

"I mean I guess almost every ancient culture has written or verbal records of a great flood but I never thought it was actually true."

"Many ancient legends have basis in reality," Gran said. His voice was so matter of fact that James just nodded and let the subject drop.

"I would like a bridge over there," he said again.

"Very well, what kind of bridge?" Gran asked.

"Ahh..." James stammered. What kind of bridge did he want, never thought that he would have to describe exactly what he wanted. "Can you make two big arches supported by a pillar in the middle of the river and with ornate railings on each side?"

"What kind of ornate markings?"

James laughed, "I don't care, can you surprise me?"

"Consider it done."

James walked to where Rose sat and lowered his body to the ground, he was careful not to sit too close to the woman. Despite his initial wariness he found that he craved the conversation and with Gran gone, Rose was all that remained.

"So have you helped all the others who came here?"

"No my mother helped Rasputin but she didn't like him very much. She said he was too close to the other side.

Now great grandma said that Merlin was very nice. He even asked her to marry him but she turned him down."

"So you and the others are born and can die at some point?"

"Yes, we have a life cycle much like humans but somewhat longer," Rose said.

James dropped the subject when she failed to explain further. Suddenly the ground under him began to shudder and out near the river cliff massive granite blocks pushed out from the banks and began a slow arching journey over the river.

"Looks like Gran is hard at work," James said. It took almost a full day and night cycle in the spirit realm for the earth spirit to finish the granite bridge and when the sun rose the next morning James stared out in amazement at the work of art before him. Solid granite beams arched out over the river with an abutment that angled down and rested on a pillar of stone driven deep into the ground under the water. Along the sides, waist high railings carved with roses and trees protected the edges without seams or fastenings.

"Amazing," James said.

"Thank you."

James jumped as the gravelly voice piped in from direct beside him. "How long would it take you to raise a wall about this high around the area?"

"I told you he would build a castle," Rose laughed. "They always do."

"Whatever," James retorted half-heartedly. Still he smiled when he looked back and saw the broad grin on her face.

"You will have to mark where you wish the walls to be," Gran said. "It will take longer to fashion walls maybe four or five days."

James nodded, tentatively he stepped onto the bridge and began walked across. "Well it certainly feels solid." He muttered.

"Why wouldn't it be?" asked Rose.

James jumped again, he had thought the spirit was back in the trees but when he turned he found her standing inches behind him.

"I don't know, I have never seen a bridge grown out of the ground before," admitted James. "It used to take my people years to build a bridge and tons of concrete."

"What's concrete?" asked Rose.

"Never mind," James replied. He spent the rest of the morning marking off the dimensions of his new home and talking with Gran about what he wanted it to look like. When he was satisfied that the spirit knew exactly what he wanted he found a place to sleep for the rest of the evening. Somehow he knew that he would be safe near the two spirits so he fell asleep quickly.

The next morning James woke up and looked directly into Rose's unblinking stare, "Ahh!" he cried and sat up suddenly. With a moment of confusion he sat up right into a branch that had grown out of the tree overnight.

"Good morning, James."

"Rose, don't do that to me," James said. Hastily he jumped to his feet and made a show of brushing the grass and twigs off his robe.

"Why?"

"Well... it just scared me," James finished lamely. The truth was that he was drawn to the spirit with her light green skin and dark hair. But how does one tell a dream that he is interested in getting to know them better, finally he just shook his head and looked to where Gran was working steadily.

"Oh, so I am scary now?" Rose laughed as she screwed up her face in a semblance of what she thought was a evil glare and stalked towards him.

Instead of looking scary James found it funny and could not stop a grin from breaking out across his face. "Maybe scared wasn't the right word. Maybe surprised would have been a better word."

Rose stopped stalking him for a moment and seemed deep in thought as she considered his words. "Alright, well, shall we go see what progress Gran has made?"

James nodded.

When they rounded the tree where James fell asleep he skidded to a halt and stared in amazement. Already the exterior walls of the inner keep rose almost to their full height and as they watched two ornate spires slowly grew from the corners of the square keep.

"Impressive," James commented as he watched. He and Rose ate a lunch of fresh fruit and nuts supplied by Rose and by lunch Gran started raising the exterior walls. While he waited James took time to explore the surrounding foothills and even ventured as far as the edge of the jagged mountains. At first he wondered where the wildlife was but the more he walked, more animals he noticed. Two spotted fawns struggled to their feet under the concerned eyes of their mother, a mile further up into the mountains he skirted a bear cub and its mother. He climbed for almost three hours before turning and looking back towards the lower lands. The view made him catch his breath, as he looked how the lands flowed together. The foothills below him stopped at the river and just beyond his growing fortress the hills gave way to a vast track of forests. The thousands of acres of trees stood strong for mile after mile until far out in the distance meadows broke the trees. He swept his eyes south and saw the line of trees bending back towards him as vast grasslands met the trees. To the north another range of jagged mountains rose into the air and dozens of snow peaked tops looked back down at him.

He explored for three days before returning to the fork in the rivers and viewing his newly completed fortress. The design he asked for worked perfectly with the surrounding cliff sides and the inner keep was a structure of beauty as well as functionality. A simple four-sided keep that rose four stories into the air and extended two floor underground. The keep was a perfect square that measured one hundred feet on each side. The curtain wall that surrounded the keep marched directly next to the cliff that dropped down to the river allowing no handholds for any would be attackers. The gatehouse was much thicker than the rest of the walls, which were in themselves nearly three feet thick. The gatehouse led directly onto the granite bridge and would make defending the castle easy if he ever needed to fight off any attackers.

"What do I do about the wood that I need?"

"Rose will have to help you with that," Gran said in a soft stately voice. "I have done all I can do here." With that statement he faded into the ground and was gone.

"Rose?" James said. He looked around wonder what tree the spirit would jump out of and not sure he wanted to find out.

"Yes?"

James whirled around trying to spot where the green tinged spirit was hiding, finally he spotted her smiling face peeking out from the leafy branches of a nearby tree.

"Gran said you could help me with timber for the roof, gate, and all the other things I will need."

"You know you could just magic most of that stuff up," Rose complained as she stepped free of the massive old oak.

James looked at the tree for a moment wondering if it had really moved away from him just slightly when he mentioned needing wood. "Yes but you know as well I do that it would take most of my energy to create that much wood. It is much easier to start with the timber available."

"Fine, but it will take me many days to gather enough timber for your needs."

James nodded, "That is alright, for some reason I think that I will be going back to the real world very soon."

"James, do not make that mistake," Rose said. Her voice was suddenly deadly serious as she looked at him with her big green eyes. "This world is just as real as earth itself. Never forget that you must keep your guard up here just as well as on earth."

He stopped and looked at her suddenly unsure of what brought the serious expression and the verbal rebuke.

"Many a wizard has decided that they were safe in this realm only to fall to the attacks of evil," Rose warned again. With those words she turned and disappeared into the forests.

James stood there for a moment and then shrugged; he would heed her words but would have to think about the warning a bit more before changing his current plans.

15 A Journey Home

James awoke with a start, his mind screaming warnings at him, he sat up quickly as his heart beat rapidly. Something was moving in the darkness. He heard the shuffling of feet fleeing up the temple steps and leaped to his feet. The globe of light erupted over his shoulder brilliantly bathing the surrounding room with light but whatever had been close to him had already disappeared.

"Alan?" James called. He glanced to where the second bed had been earlier but it was gone and there was no sign of Dr. Alan Stewart. Either the other man had fled or something had taken him.

"I wonder if I will ever see him again." With a wave of his hand he got rid of the bed and mattress, somewhere in his mind he knew that he would not need it again. The next time he was forced to sleep for any length of time he would do it somewhere else. He looked around the central chamber one last time when something caught his eye.

"He left the codex, how odd." James retrieved the ancient codex and slipped it into his pack. He took his blanket and whatever odds and ends he had created over the past years and packed them carefully into the leather pack then he slipped it over his shoulder and retrieved his staff from where it leaned against a nearby wall.

The steps out of the temple were dusty except for a single set of tracks that he assumed were some sort of animals. The footprint was round and contained scratch marks that could have only come from sharp claws. At the entrance to the temple he paused to rebuild the wall that blocked entrance to the structure. Once he exited the temple he went so far as to rebuild the second wall and to remove many traces that marked the entry. Then he climbed to the top of the hill and looked around, the rocky slopes of the distant volcano were now covered in greenery and many small trees now sprouted almost all the way to the cone.

"Must have slept a long time," James muttered. He was torn between going south to check in on Javier's people and traveling north to where he had grown up in Minnesota. Finally he turned south and began walking.

Three days later he exited the jungle and looked down at the bustling city below him on the fertile plain. Three long piers now stretched out into the water and dozens of fishing boats were tied off to the wooden posts. A rough stockade surrounded much of the city and James figured that the city now covered nearly five acres. He counted several hundred small figures moving around the gravel streets and dozens more working in the fields. Satisfied that all was well he turned back to the jungle and walked east until he reached the ocean. For a time he just ambled, enjoying the warm sand and soft breeze that drifted in off the ocean.

On the beach around him crabs occasionally scuttled away from him and in the shallow pools small fish waited for the coming tide to provide them a way back to the deep water. He walked when he felt like it and rested when he felt tired. The sun was warm and no sense of urgency filled him. Things had changed on planet earth and he wanted to move slowly at first and discover what was different and what remained the same.

It was late evening when he found the ruined remains of an old sailing boat pushed up almost into the jungle. He was so excited that in ten minutes he was able to shove off from the beach and raised the remade sail over the magically repaired hull. Thankfully he still felt rested despite the amount of power he expended and that gave him more confidence.

"Just like new," James said with a smile. The winds were shifting slowly so he rolled up his robe and put it in his pack. He slipped on a pair of Bermuda shorts that cost a bit of energy to create from almost nothing and sat back to enjoy the sun.

He kept a minor shield in place above the boat to ward off the direct effects of the sun and then sat back watching the coasts slip by. It was near evening the next day when he spotted the rusted remains of a massive cruise ship run aground about fifty yards from shore. He circled the ship once wondering if it was worth going aboard, finally he tied his small sailboat and willed his body into the air until he stood on the sloped deck. Almost half of the deck was intact but near the bow something had ripped a massive gash that extended down under the water line.

"Hello?" James called as he stepped into the cavernous dining hall. The crystal chandeliers still hung from the ceiling looking down at the skeletal remains of passengers and crew. He gathered a few articles of clothing that remained and used his power to restore the cloth to a new condition. He even found a tube of sun block that had hardened completely. Lifting the sun block thoughtfully he concentrated on it wondering if it were possible. Moments later he held a restored tube and squeezed a generous dab into his hands. Back on deck he rubbed the sun block into his skin and slipped back over the side to his sailboat.

"No more need for the shield."

He allowed the shield to drop and untied the line holding his boat to the remains of the ship. Slowly the ship faded until it was lost from sight and only the jungle filled coasts greeted his eyes. His sailboat was nearly twenty-eight feet in length and it had a comfortable cabin below decks. When night fell and the stars looked down at him he navigated closer to shore and dropped anchor. After making sure the boat was secure he entered the cabin and moved about fixing the things he had overlooked the first time. The bed was small but it fit him well enough and he created enough blankets to keep him warm even if the nights turned much colder. The silence of the night was broken only by the occasional tapping of waves against the hull and instead of sitting in the solitude and dreaming of days gone by he welcomed it using the time to make a cursory examination of the codex.

The first two chapters contained information about the upper levels of the temple and he read with interest as the stiff pages described the materials put into the upper rooms and the names of the men and women who designed and oversaw the construction. The third chapter started delving into the lower rooms and James began finding many words he could not decipher. Finally, after his fifth yawn, he set the codex carefully in his pack, rolled up in his blanket, and dropped off to sleep.

The next morning greeted him with calm seas and beautiful sunshine again so he took a quick dip in the ocean and then reapplied his sun block.

He traveled north for nearly a week according to the compass built into the boat. Occasionally he spotted the remains of coastal towns now almost completely reclaimed by the jungles. It was morning of the eighth day when the coasts suddenly turned west and faded into the distance.

"Must have just cleared the Yucatan peninsula," James muttered. It looked to be only mid-afternoon but he dropped anchor near shore and spent the afternoon resting under the shade palms. There was a thick gathering of clouds out in the Gulf of Mexico and he had no wish to be caught in a storm.

The next morning the storm seemed to move off to the east so he boarded his small sailboat and raised the anchor. Rather then slowly continuing to work his way along the coasts James turned north and also drifted a bit west as he started running diagonally across the gulf. At first the idea seemed good, he hoped he would cut days off his journey and if his memory was right arrive along the Texas coasts.

The first two days went by smoothly with stiff winds pushing him along quickly, then the sea turned calm and his sails drifted listlessly from side to side. After two days of calm in which the currents moved his small boat much further north then he intended, he spotted a dot of green far to the north and a bit east.

"That is too soon to be the US, and I don't remember any islands in the gulf."

Rather than fight the currents he reefed his sails and let the water pull him along until he was about a hundred yards from the strange coast. When he thought he was close enough, he dumped the anchor over the side and floated up into the air to survey the entire isle. It was small, maybe five thousand yards wide, twice that in length, and fashioned almost like a horseshoe. Two rugged hills dominated the end of the shoe and the rest of it was filled with trees and a variety of plants that must have been carried in on the currents or on the wind. The isle was strangely quiet, only the chirping of a few birds and the hum of insects brought any noise.

James dropped back to his sailboat and raised the sail; off to the east a row of thunderclouds filled the horizon. They were not visible from the surface but he guessed they would arrive soon. Thankfully the advancing storms brought with them a fresh wind and soon he was racing ahead of the storm. On a whim he lightened his ship in the same way he did with his body when he floated into the air and soon he was moving at tremendous speed.

Two days of racing before the storm and James was ready to stop, his stomach was in his throat and he had not eaten or slept since leaving the strange isle. He was about to give up and let the storm catch him when a brown and green coastline came into view. As he raced towards the land it spread in each direction out of sight, "Texas at last!" he cried.

He gave the boat its weight back slowly as he approached land and then swung his tiller north to track with the coasts. The storm passed to the south and all he received was an hour or so of rain until the skies began to clear.

After a day of moving north and a bit east along the coast apprehension began to fill him. Inland about a mile from the coasts massive pillars of rock and dirt rose hundreds of feet into the air and the smell of sulfur made his nose wrinkle again and again. They reminded him of ant colonies but hundreds of times bigger then anything he had ever seen.

"Whatever happened, the Texas I knew is no longer there," James said. He talked now just to hear the sound of his own voice. Despite becoming more adjusted to the solitude that filled the earth now he still craved sound.

It was morning on the third day and clouds of black smoke bellowed almost constantly from the stone pillars.

When he could take it no longer James was forced to move out from the coasts further to avoid passing out from the volatile gasses that filled the air. They made his eyes water and brought hacking coughs from him every time he caught a whiff of the gasses.

It was late that day when he spotted the eyeless creature watching from the ruined coast. In the distance a massive column of stone filled the air billowing black clouds. He recognized the area he was in despite the century of decay that had taken its toll.

"Galveston, so much for the city."

Suddenly a movement drew his eye and he directed his boat closer to the coasts, there on the beach a dozen or more antlike creatures scuttled along the sands feeling the ground with long antenna and snapping fierce looking pinchers. He watched for a while trying to catalogue the things in his mind but finally gave up. They varied some in size but even the smallest was larger then a horse.

"They look like a cross between an ant and a crab but twisted and evil looking."

By this time he had drifted to within about fifty feet of shore and the things on the beach froze the moment he spoke. Immediately they approached the water line and began testing the edge of the water with their feelers.

Apparently they have great hearing James thought as he kept his mouth firmly shut.

He willed his small craft to be silent and then pulled on the rudder until he was a good hundred yards off shore. As he watched the creatures turned back to their sweep of the shore and then finally scuttled off towards the pillars. Unable to move to shore he drifted along for over a day trying to count the pillars and then finally stopping. Once he drifted high into the sky but found that his view of the surrounding countryside was completely cut off. As he drifted away from Galveston the concentration of the creature's hills lessened until finally they faded from view and open prairie replaced the destruction around central Texas. Nearly four weeks passed before James spotted any sign of human habitation. Scattered along the coasts were numerous shipwrecks in various states of decay and each time James stopped to do a quick survey of the rusted wrecks. Each time only silence and animals greeted his arrival and witnessed his departure.

It wasn't until he reached the swamps near New Orleans that he spotted the first sign of people and by this time he was eager to talk to anyone. A broad low coastal island stretched out for miles near where the Mississippi River Delta entered the gulf. With the human influence gone and the city fallen into complete decay the river once again claimed its own. Coastal islands reformed and protected the marshes fed by silt from the mighty Mississippi River.

"Should have left it alone after Hurricane Katrina," mused James with a sad smile on his face. He approached the city near dusk and anchored well offshore not sure who or what was living in the area or even if they would find his presence threatening.

The next morning was overcast but no rain came so James moved his sailboat in a bit closer until he finally located the channel that he believed was the mighty river. Silently he slipped his small boat in the channel and worked the sail until he caught the wind well enough to begin fighting up river against the current. Within the first hour James realized that he could not be able to go on as he planned, the current was so strong and for every ten feet he gained he slipped back five. Finally he lightened the craft again and skimmed north almost atop the surface. The remains of the city watched his passage, frowning at the ant of a man who dared disturb their long slumber. To James's amazement many of the buildings remained standing despite the passage of nearly a century. He spotted the remains of the Super Dome with ease even though much of the material that once formed the top was now rotted away but the structure itself still stood shrouded in vines.

Two hours later the remnants of New Orleans faded into the distance and James began to get the feeling he was being watched. Flashes of movement caught his eye but when he tried to check a glimpse of the elusive watcher it vanished. A flash of tanned skin glimpsed through a gap between two trees or the scuff of material rubbing against the enclosing leaves of a thick wall of bushes. Finally he dropped anchor in the widest part of the river and slipped his shield down over his body. This time though he willed the shield to reflect the nearby trees, finally he slipped overboard and floated towards shore.

Even from his vantage point high in the air it took him nearly ten minutes to finally spot the group of watchers. Not surprising, he spotted seven different people hidden along the riverbank watching his now silent and still craft. Three were armed with crude but serviceable spears while two toted older but well maintained shotguns. The last couple held bows and full quivers of arrows. Even more ominous was the fact that five of the watchers wore necklaces that appeared to contain human finger bones. People had survived but he doubted that this group was one with which he wanted to sit down to dinner.

James waited until the small group gathered and seemed to confer about the lack of movement on the sailboat. Finally after nearly an hour they trooped back into the swamps and were soon lost from sight. After waiting another ten minutes he started to move back towards the river when he spotted another person hidden in the rushes that covered the banks of the river. She was young maybe twenty at most and so covered in dirt and mud that he nearly missed seeing her. If she had not moved just as he paused to check his surrounding he would have not seen her at all. Rather then make his presence known he waited silently and watched.

Soon she poked her head out of the rushes and slipped from her hiding place. After pausing to listen for nearly five minutes she walked to a sandy section of riverbank and washed her face cleaning away the layers of grime. When the riverbank remained quiet she leaned down to the river was about to take a drink when the watchers returned. Whoops and cries filled the air as the seven returned scrambling through the brushes.

From his perch James saw the fear erupt in her eyes and he swooped lower wanting to be in place for what he assumed would soon be a needed rescue. On the sandy beach the woman dove into the water and tried to reach the depths of the river but she could not swim well and was soon dragged kicking and screaming onto the sand. Several were sharpening knives as they looked at her and one even licked his lips hungrily.

James floated even closer until only a dozen feet separated him from the group standing over the frightened girl. He knew he had to work quickly so he focused on the firearms first. The thought had not occurred to him that guns might still work and the danger they would pose to him would be significant. On a whim he focused on the weapons barrels until small light plugs of metal filled each of them. They might fire but they would explode in the faces of the raiders. When he was satisfied that all he would face was the lesser weapons he dropped his shield and remained hovering about ten feet off the ground.

16 Cate

A collective gasp erupted from the encircling raiders and the young woman fainted to the ground. Seven sets of eyes stared at him in utter and complete shock and James glared back, his white robe shining brilliantly in the light of the sun. One of the raiders carrying a shotgun with a dark barrel slowly raised the weapon to his shoulder and took aim. James watched the movement with interest, obviously the man with his rotten teeth and grimy hair had not noticed the added weight of the iron plug. On a whim James strengthened his protective shield in front of the gun and smiled benignly.

"Keel heem," screeched the gun wielder. His ratted cut-off jeans were covered in blood stains and the human bones that pierced his ears and cheeks shook wildly as he cried out for his companions to attack. He pulled the trigger on his shotgun with a smirk that said he was going to soon feast on human flesh.

James found it impossible to not jump at least a bit when the shotgun went off with a puff of black powder and then exploded in a cloud of shrapnel. The hot lead and weakened steel from the barrel cut down two of the raiders and the blowback from the plugged barrel sent the shooter flying backwards into the shallow water where he rested quietly much of his face missing. The remaining four men scrambled to their feet and scattered into the swamps running as fast as they could through the tangled underbrush. Moments later the riverbank was quiet and James dropped down to the sand and walked to where the woman lay still on the sand. The waves from the river lapped at her face and as James knelt on the sand her eyes snapped open.

"Wait, it's alright," James said gently. He held his hands up in a sign of surrender. The young woman who he assumed was in her mid twenties stared at him with wild eyes and began to edge away, her eyes darting to the nearby water. "Please don't run I am not going to hurt you. I just want to talk to someone."

"The Cajune will be back," she said as her eyes flickered to the deserted line of trees.

James signed with relief as she seemed to relax and a smile spread across his face at her perfect if slightly southern accented English. "What is your name?"

"Cate."

"Well Cate I have a boat anchored out in the water and we can be far upriver by time they return if you would join me."

Cate eyed him warily, she seemed to be trying to decide if she wanted to take the chance with the Cajune or him. Finally she nodded and looked at him, "Do we swim out to it?"

"No, I will bring it in," James said. Carefully he used his power to bring the anchor up from the bottom and then directed the boat towards them. As he concentrated he glanced at Cate and saw she was staring at him with fear in her eyes.

"My parents never told me that there were people like you in the world before the heavens burned," Cate whispered.

"There were not," admitted James. The sailboat slid into the shallows past the bulrushes and finally ground to a halt next to where they waited. In the air to the south James heard the scattered shouts that heralded the return of the Cajune in greater numbers. "We should go."

Cate nodded and she jumped over the side of the boat, she seated herself stiffly on the only padded seat and waited for James. He glanced east and then climbed aboard himself, with a shove of his foot he sent the lighter then usual boat back out into the water and slipped the sail loose of the mast. They caught the slight breeze and with the weight of the boat abated the small skiff went racing north across the water despite the sluggish current driving inevitably south.

"How are you doing that?" Cate asked finally. With a grateful smile she accepted the damp towel and began to wipe her face and arms clean of the dried mud.

"Doing what?" James was amazed to find that she was a very beautiful woman with blue eyes and dirty blond hair. Despite the absence of modern dentistry her teeth were perfectly formed and the hint of a smile played around her mouth for the merest of moments.

"There is little wind and yet we are racing like a full gale was blowing in from the ocean," Cate commented. "I may not know much of sailing but I know that such a thing should not be possible."

"It is a gift given to me a long time ago, James said evasively. "What do you remember of the meteor shower?" The confused look on her face showed him he would have to explain further. He wracked his mind and then remembered what she had said earlier then it came to him. "The day the sky burned. What do you know of it?"

"Our legends say that god grew angry at the way people were living on earth. They say he sent great stones to wipe out the evil that filled our land. My father told me that his father survived the day the sky burned because he lived right but I don't believe it. I think he was lucky."

James smiled at her sarcastic tone and nodded, "I saw what happened that day, and for those that survived sheer luck was all that mattered. My friend and I were deep underground and we managed to survive."

"How could you have seen it?" Cate demanded. She folded her arms and glared at him suspiciously. "It was many years ago, you are not old enough to have seen it." Suspicion filled her eyes and she once again began searching for the quickest escape route available to her.

"I found something that changed me. I slept for many years and survived..." he held up his hands to silence her. "I don't understand how it all happened. All I know is that it happened. I saw the great meteors as they burned their horrible trails of destruction across the sky. When one struck near us, when we saw what was happening we went deep underground."

She seemed skeptical of the explanation but did relax some.

"So where did you grow up, how have you survived?" James asked.

"My family grew up just north of here in the forests near Atlan," Cate explained. "There was a small village and we lived in peace until the Cajune pushed into our territory. They attacked our village and killed most of the people. I ran as fast as I could and they chased me down to the river."

"Did anyone else survive?" James asked.

"No, I don't think so," Cate admitted. Suddenly the collected tension of the last days seemed to catch her and she burst into tears. Burying her face in the soiled towel her shoulders shook as the sobs broke loose.

"It's alright Cate, we all lost people we loved recently," James said softly. Carefully he sat down beside her and gently touched her shoulder. He wanted to comfort her but he also did not want to scare her into jumping into the river. Thankfully she seemed to sense his hesitancy and she set her head against his shoulder and cried into his shoulder. Deep sobbing shook her and James carefully put his arm around her and gently patted the back of her head. When her crying had run its course she pulled back from his arm and wiped the remaining tears from her eyes.

"Thank you."

"It's alright," James said quietly. He stood and walked back to where his small stock of food was packed in a wooden crate. With a flip of the lid he removed the assortment of fruit and vegetables and motioned with his hand. "Would you like something to eat?"

She nodded and removed an apple and an orange, as the riverbank continued to slip by they ate in silence listening for any sign that the Cajune were trying to keep pace with them.

"Where are the Cajune from?" James asked. He didn't want to keep bringing up the past but he needed more information about the condition of the former United States.

"I know that they came from the southern swamps but before that I am not sure. Before this week I had never seen them, just heard rumors from travelers. Warnings to not enter the deep southern swamps because of the cannibals."

James nodded, "Are there rumors of survivors anywhere else?"

"Some spoke of larger towns that have been rebuilt further to the north and far to the east. No one travels west, only death exists in the Great Plains to the west."

"Yes, I think I saw some of them from the shore," James said. "Hideous looking creatures, a twisting of nature into things that look like creatures I have never seen before. Does anyone know where they came from?"

"Rumors say they came from the earth. It was said that they were part of god's judgment against the earth."

James shrugged; it was good that she had heard of larger human settlements to the north. In his mind he knew that he planned to travel all the way to where the state of Minnesota had formerly been located. It might be possible to contact some of these survivors.

"So how does news travel now?" James asked. He still lacked even the most basic understanding of how life was conducted in the lands around him and he desperately wanted to know more.

"We hardly ever had news from outside our village. Now and then a traveling trader would visit and sell goods from the bigger towns to the north but even then the news was months old." Cate paused for a moment and then continued, "My father was a farmer and my mother was a seamstress. From what my father told me, and his grandfather told him, the world used to be a very different place. Sometimes we find things left over from before but none of it ever works. Sometimes father would tell me about panes of glass that would have pictures playing on them and mirrors with numbers on them. None of it ever works."

"Yes, I have a theory about that but haven't had a chance to prove any of it," James muttered. The sun was beginning to set in the western sky and James directed the boat towards shore not wanting to take the chance of running into hidden rocks and logs by running at night.

"Have you ever been through this area?" James asked.

"No, our village was farther north and closer to the ruins of a big city. What a city it must have been, we visited the edge of it one time searching for things to help us harvest. Hundreds of square houses built of wood. Many of them are now rotten but some have survived. Windows with glass that is so clear you can see right through it like it really isn't there."

James let her talk sensing that she just wanted to vent emotions that needed to be released. He puttered about the boat arranging a sleeping area for himself and then he set out a tray of fruit, vegetables, and nuts. They ate quietly watching the sky turn hues of orange and red and Cate seemed to have vented all that she needed. When they were done eating James cleaned off the few dishes that he had salvaged. As darkness surrounded them, he nodded to the small cabin built into the hull.

"You can sleep down there in the bed. I will sleep up here on the deck," James said. He waved off her objections, "You have given me more tonight then I could have ever asked for."

Cate made her way down the narrow steps to the cabin and slid the thin door shut while James was arranging his blankets. When he felt all was ready he slipped under the blanket and stared up at the stars. It had been years since he had seen the sky so big and so bright. In the years before his trip to Guatemala the sky was muted, filled with light that went up from the cities and blocked the views of the stars. In fact, he did not remember the last time when he had simply lain down and looked at the stars. The moon rose slowly, dimming his view of the Big Dipper and Orion so he turned on his side and closed his eyes willing sleep to come quickly.

The next morning dawned with a dark sky and James came awake with a start, in his mind alarm bells were ringing and he froze to listen. Silence filled the world all around him and that alone told him something was wrong, no chirping of birds echoed off the water, no insects buzzed about him trying to get passed his barrier. Slowly James lifted his head and looked around; it took him a minute to spot the motionless figure standing on shore. Covered in a dull brown armor the antlike creature stared at the small boat with beady black eyes. Tentatively it tested the water but it seemed reluctant to enter the river. James tried to probe it with his new found power but all he saw was a spot of blackness, curiously he turned and probed the cabin where Cate was sleeping and was able to spot her life sign immediately. Unlike the dark spot where the creature stood her body was marked by a soft reddish spot lying on the small bunk.

James turned back and saw the ant creature had finally worked up its courage enough to enter the shallow water and was now only about five yards from where the boat was anchored. He cast about for some way to stop the creature when one of the fantasy movies that he watched years ago came to mind. With a shrug he pointed his finger at the creature and focused. Seconds later a ball of fire erupted from his hand and flew across the water. The fire slammed into the monster and stuck to it burning it to death in moments.

As the ant monster died it clacked its pincers loudly three times and then slipped below the surface of the water.

"How did you do that?"

James jumped as Cate asked the question from directly behind him. "One of the little tricks I picked up lately." James smiled and motioned to where the ant creature's carapace still stuck just barely above the water level. "Is that the creatures that you said came from the ground?"

"Yes they kill everything that they come across and drag it off to deep tunnels delved into the earth," Cate said. She took an apple from the small box of food and then eyed the dwindling supply. "How do you get your food?"

"I have ways," replied James absently. His attention was still locked on the western shore.

"I want what you have," said Cate quietly. When he failed to respond he repeated it. "I want what you have!" This time she said it with a much more determined tone in her voice. "I want that magic or whatever it is."

This time James turned to look at her unsure of what to say. Finally he when he did speak it was with great hesitancy. "Cate, I slept for nearly a hundred years as my body and mind changed. It is a long process and the only place where it can take happen is far away. I must visit my former home before I even consider returning to Guatemala."

"I have nothing to lose, James. I will stay with you until you are able to return to where it is. I do not care if it takes me the rest of my life."

"I would welcome the company," James replied. "But I make no promises."

"Fine," Cate nodded as though she had decided the situation was now closed. "What do we do now?"

"North," James said. He smiled as she crossed to the anchor and began pulling the anchor free of the mud. When the anchor was again stowed just under the lip of the prow he loosened the ties on the canvas sail and lightened the boat enough to send it racing north again.

For nearly five days they traveled north, following the flow of the river. They camped each night under the stars and spent the evenings watching for any sign of civilization. James spent a good part of one day creating a map from memory that marked most of the main locations of the cities along the

Mississippi River. On the third day as he was adding two numbers together on a scrap of paper he noticed the confused look on Cate face.

"Can you read or write?" James asked.

"Yes I can read a little and my father taught me my letters but I have had little chance to practice."

"What about numbers?"

"Those I do not know," murmured Cate. Her face turned bright red with embarrassment as she admitted her lack of knowledge.

"Well, sit down, Cate." James motioned to the deck beside him. With a wave of his hand he created a stack of paper and a thick pencil. "Take these and I will help you learn how to add and subtract at least."

A brilliant smile lit Cate's face as she excitedly picked up the pencil and arranged the papers in a tight stack before her. They spent the rest of the day moving north along the river and with James teaching Cate how to write numbers and reviewing what she knew of the alphabet.

Six days later James figured they had entered the foothills of northern Kentucky or maybe even southern Ohio. It was early evening and the sun was still riding high in the sky when James spotted the telltale plumes of smoke rising high in the air to the west.

"Cate, look," James pointed. "Smoke, that means there are people in that direction."

"Want to go see who they are?" Cate asked. Over the last few days her quick mind grasped all the concepts of math James gave her and they had even moved into multiplication and division. The initial fear that existed between them faded and Cate now felt comfortable around the mysterious robed figure that wielded such power.

"I think it is worth checking into," James agreed. "But first we need to find a way to protect you." James turned and looked at her closely trying to decide what to do. She was a beautiful woman and he assumed would draw attention from the men everywhere. Finally he picked up one of the shirts he had salvaged from the cruise ship and concentrated on the fibers of the cloth. Carefully he began creating and weaving threads into the shirt that were harder then steel but ten times lighter. When he was done he handed it to her and waited while she stepped into the cabin and slipped the shirt on.

James laughed when she emerged with the baggy shirt hanging loosely around her torso, "Hold still I think I can fix that." While she waited he molded the shirt to her body trying not to concentrate too closely on the trim body under the shirt. When he was done the black shirt fit tightly to her body and left little to imagination but when she shrugged back into her other clothes the armor was hidden perfectly. James was happy to find that the extensive work with magic he was doing was not draining his strength completely. It took another half hour to create a matching pair of pants and when they finally put ashore the sun was riding very low in the sky.

17 The Preacher

The town that they looked out on some twenty minutes later was a model of a late medieval village if James had ever seen one. A thick palisade of heavy logs were cut, set into the ground, and tied together at the top. After that, a second and third row of timbers formed a walkway just inside the main wall. James hunkered down behind a thick stand of brush and watched the people walk around the dirt streets below him. He and Cate were well hidden on a low hill almost two hundred yards away so they were able to see some of what was going on inside the village. The houses were built of timber and roofed with tar covered timber slats; the placement of the dwellings was very close together thereby packing more people into the confines of the town.

"It looks like they are expanding to the north," Cate said. She motioned in the mentioned direction.

James followed her pointed finger to where almost two-dozen men were in the process of setting another timber into an expansion of the exterior wall. "Obviously they have problems with someone or they wouldn't be expending so much effort building a defensive position. Look around, the forests are cut back almost two hundred yards everywhere that we can see and they have people watching in all directions." James pointed out the precautions that the people were taking.

"Shall we make our presence known?" asked Cate. She turned and regard James with her pale blue eyes, as she waited she brushed a stray lock of hair back from her face and tucked it behind her left ear.

"Might as well," James said. He handed her a powerful longbow that he constructed over the last twenty minutes by bonding the wood and adding as much spring to the wood as he dared. By the time he had finished he was sure the bow would pull fairly easily but it would send an arrow a hundred yards with enough power to punch through most armor. "Have you used a bow before?"

"Many times," Cate said. "My father took me hunting all the time."

"Good, I can't shoot straight enough to hit the broad side of a barn," laughed James as he handed her the matching quiver of arrows. He waited until she had comfortably fitted the quiver around her shapely hips and seemed comfortable and then he stood to his feet. After adjusting his robes he smiled to himself and stepped out on top of the hill in full view of the town. Next to him Cate adjusted her wide brimmed hat and then carefully set one of the shafts against the bow and notched into the string then she stepped out beside him with the bow pointed away from the town.

Almost immediately an alarm bell began ringing and many figures began scurrying around the town. James walked slowly and made sure he kept the tall hood tossed back so that anyone who watched would be able to see that he was human. Beside him he thought Cate looked almost like a cowboy with a long cloak and a bow instead of a rifle.

"I wonder if we can find any rifles that survived the impacts," mused James as they walked to where a well-worn path led a straight route to the closed gate.

"Rifles?" questioned Cate.

"Like the shotguns that the Cajune were using but made for long range."

"I have never seen anything like that before," Cate said. She stopped talking as a voice called from the wall in front of them drawing their attention.

They were about seventy-five yards from the walls when a voice rang out challenging them.

"That be far nuff."

James stopped and nodded amiably to the row of figures that glared at them from the top of the fifteen-foot wall. He doubted that fortifications would stop the ant creatures but it would surely stop any human attackers.

"Whadya want."

"We are simple travelers looking for a place to stay for the night," James called. He almost hadn't understood the question with the thickness of the southern accent that filled the speaker's voice.

"They have weapons pointed at us."

James nodded as he noticed the same thing that Cate so quietly pointed out, "I would if I were them also."

"Whadya have to trade."

"It might help us if I were able to approach the gate and speak to you face to face without having to yell," James called hoping that the spokesman would agree.

"Leave the bow and the staff."

James nodded he set his staff carefully on the ground and then motioned for Cate to stay where she was for now. "If I call out just run. I can protect himself easier if I know you're safe." The words came out with more feeling then he wanted and he saw a small smile play across Cate's face as she nodded and stepped back a few feet.

James walked to spot about ten feet before the timber gate and waited as the people pulled whatever locking mechanism held the big doors shut and opened them just enough for a tall thin man with a scraggly beard to slip out.

"I donna see any trade goods."

"Look, my companion and I have not seen anyone in almost two weeks and we saw smoke from the river. We were hoping to collect some news before we move on. We mean no harm," James said again. "All we came with was the clothes on our backs and my staff and her bow."

"Well, my name is Billbob and we don't let just anyone into Kentuck," Billbob said. "Preacher would have to clear you."

"Can we speak to him?" James asked.

"Rip!" Billbob called. A moment later another bearded face popped up over the wall. "Go tell preacher we gots guests at the gate."

"Alighty," Rip answered and then he disappeared from view.

James waited for almost five minutes until another man stepped out from the gate and walked to where he and Billbob stood in awkward silence. When he spoke James breathed a sigh of relief.

"Now then, what have we here?"

The Preacher's voice was quiet and cultured and James took an immediately liking to him. "We have a boat on the river and saw the smoke from the village. We were hoping for a place to stay for the night and maybe news of happenings around the area."

"Are you a believer?"

The question took James by surprise, He frowned for a moment and suddenly a small cloud of doubt appeared for a moment on the horizon of his mind. After a brief but awkward silence a wide grin broke across the Preachers face and he laughed uproariously.

"It's alright, the few travelers that come this way expect to be filled with good preachin. It was more of a test to see if you had really ever been in these parts before. By the blank look on your face I will assume that you haven't."

James nodded and let a smile slip through his suddenly increased defenses in his mind, "No, we outran a group down south called the Cajune and have been traveling the river against the current for many weeks." James felt the need to hide exactly how long they had been traveling, all the better not to have to answer too many questions about how they had traveled so far so quickly.

"Hmm about a year ago a family came up from the deep south. They mentioned a group of cannibals by that name. You were lucky to survive."

"A few days ago we saw a horrible creature on the river bank," James offered in the way of news. "It was hideous, looked like an ant crossed with a crab."

"Ah, you have seen the colony scouts. They have been pushing north again lately. We have been forced to keep a heavy watch to the south and west even to the detriment of our fields."

"Do you have a name for them?" James asked as he began to relax again around the amiable man.

"We call them Satan's children, they are scavengers killing and carrying everything they can away to the bowels of earth. It is said that their holes reach to the depths of hell itself." The Preacher stopped and let a dramatic pause hang in the air for a moment then he smiled. "Of course, I have never known anyone who was able to return from their tunnels and confirm that last bit."

They shook hands and the Preacher motioned to where Cate still waited silently with her bow ready to fire at the moment's notice. "Tell your mysterious friend to gather up your staff and you may join us for our evening meal. God will surely bless us for sharing with such needy travelers."

James nodded and motioned for Cate to approach.

"Is she your wife?" the Preacher asked suddenly. It was almost as if he had just noticed that Cate was a woman and a young beautiful woman at that.

James nodded in what he hoped was a noncommittal way. He found himself wishing it were true but not wanting to admit to anyone that it wasn't. Cate was about twenty feet away and he was not sure if she had heard the question so he tried to catch her eye in warning.

"Thanks for leaving me out in the cold, my love," Cate grumbled. She winked at him in a conspiratorial manner letting him know she had followed the conversation.

James almost fell over when she stopped and kissed him lightly on the lips, but her mouth felt good so he slipped an arm around her and enjoyed the moment. "I am sorry my dear, but they said to approach unarmed and you know me. I would have forgotten where I left my staff the moment I set it down."

Then in a low voice that only she could hear he whispered in her ear, "Thanks for playing along. Something is strange here I just can't put my finger on it. Keep your eyes open."

She nodded and smiled brilliantly to him then turned to the Preacher and offered him an almost dainty curtsy as she slipped the arrow back into its quiver.

"My lady, seldom are we blessed with such beauty, truly you are a angel sent from heaven itself to brighten the world." The Preacher took her hand and brushed it lightly to his lips as he spoke.

Oh, he was a smooth one, this preacher, James thought to himself. Still, as James looked on he felt a tiny surge of jealousy directed at the Preacher but it faded quickly when the suave man released Cate's hand.

"Open the gate," the Preacher ordered. He led them through and then motioned for the portal to be closed. "Reset the watch and then get those last few timbers in place." The cluster of men nodded at his orders and then scattered across the village.

James took a moment to examine the surroundings of the town closely while they waited for the Preacher to finish arranging the gate watch to his liking. The village was closer to a town in size then he realized from the hilltop. He estimated that nearly two hundred homes filled the timber walls and a fair number of businesses ranging from a blacksmith to a tanner.

"Now then, my friends, let us retreat to my dwelling and we can pick each others minds about the wide world around us."

James nearly jumped when a smallish hand slipped into his as they turned to follow the Preacher across town. As they trailed after the black suited man Cate clung to his hand doing her best to act like a loving wife and James found that he enjoyed it. He was still saddened by the thought that his wife Carol had died by herself, with him far away. Despite the pain he was pragmatic enough to realize that she was long gone and it would do him little good to cling to her memory too tightly. In actual time it had been a century and he would have to learn to move on without her.

The Preacher's home was built onto the back of the biggest building in town and as James expected, the building was a church. The sign over the door read Kentuck Chapel of the Azores.

"The Azores Mountains," James said. "Is that where we are?"

"Yes, well, kind of on the edge of them. Many things changed when god sent his judgment against the earth. Mountains moved, as did the course of some rivers. The people in this area were fortunate to be a god-fearing people and he spared them much of his wrath. Few of the great rocks fell through this area and more survived here than anywhere I have visited."

"You have traveled?" asked James.

"Yes some, we have led scouting parties almost ten days in every direction. There are a few small outposts to the east deeper in the mountains but many of the survivors gathered here. There was a town from the old days located here and a source of fresh water so it seemed logical for our ancestors to stay."

"It seems that your people are prospering," James commented as they entered a small one-room cabin. A second door led into the back of the church and it was open enough that James was able to see an altar and small lectern with a massive volume sitting on it.

"Yes, we have been blessed thus far. We also have the fortune of being atop one of the few surviving coal mines in this area," the Preacher said. The black clad man crossed to the door leading to the chapel and swung it closed then motioned to the rough table and chairs. "Please be seated and tell me of your travels."

James sat down on the rough surface and he was surprised to feel his inner sense of danger screaming warnings at him, the small hairs on the back of his neck stood on end. So on edge was he that when a small scratching sound echoed out of the chapel he nearly spilled the cup of tea offered to him.

"Well there you're about as jumpy as a chicken in the fox den. Something wrong?" the Preacher asked. He smiled amicably and then turned back to the wood stove that sat in one corner. It was built of blackened iron and reminded James of a tiny image of what the gates of hell might look like. With his back turned he took a long stick and stirred the coals as he blew lightly on them, when a tiny flame finally erupted he fed some small bits of wood into the belly of the beast.

Morbidly James watched the fire as it grew in size and began consuming the pieces of coal that the Preacher slipped into it. Cate seemed to have caught his feeling of unease because she sat wide-eyed looking at him for some hint of trouble. With a grimace James motioned for her to sit quietly and then he turned his senses back to the Preacher who was pulling out the chair opposite him.

"Now then, tell me some tales of what goes on outside our little piece of heaven," the Preacher smiled widely. "Many would consider our life a bit simple but we have all that we really need. I always say paradise or hell it's all a state of mind, wouldn't you say James?"

James nodded, he opened his mouth to speak when the scratching sound from the chapel erupted into what sounded like the rattling of iron bars.

"Ugh, excuse me for just one moment good folks," the Preacher said. Carefully he rose from his seat and placed his teacup on the table. Then he walked into the roughly built chapel building. Moments later he was completely out of sight on the far side of the building and James looked at Cate.

"Something is wrong here," James hissed softly. "I don't know what or where but something strange is going on and I mean to find out what. Just be ready if trouble starts."

Cate nodded she retrieved her bow and quiver from the corner and began removing and checking each shaft in turn looking for problems but also giving her access to the razor sharp arrows. From the chapel came the sound of a metal striking metal and an inarticulate shout that brought James to his feet and took him three steps toward the door.

Suddenly the Preacher stood framed in the door carrying a heavy iron bar, his hair was disheveled and his breath came in rasping gasps as though he had run miles.

"Where are you going?"

"We heard shouts and thought something was wrong," James countered. He examined the chapel over the shoulder of the black clad man. There were ten rows of rough benches that stretched from wall to wall with a single walkway dividing them down the center. Two matched panes of glass and the last rays of the dying sun illuminated the area and near the front of the chapel opened a yawning hole leading down into the earth.

"Where does that lead?" James asked.

"To our coal mine of course, god giveth and he taketh away, so what better place to place our house of worship but over the very life blood of our town." The Preacher smiled and motioned for them to return to the table in his small sleeping area.

"I don't think so Preacher, I think my companion and I are going to return to our boat," James said. His fear had temporarily abated and a bit of steel entered into him and more then a little curiosity.

"That my friend is impossible. For you see once someone enters our little piece of heaven they may not leave.

And indeed, why would any want to leave when we can offer so much. A home will be set-aside for you and your lovely lady friend. You may take your rest there and then come here to the chapel to be assigned a job and to defend your right to possess a lady of such extraordinary beauty."

The Preacher's eyes took on a slightly vacant look and he tried to shove by James to reach out and touch Cate's face.

"Have you lost it?" James demanded. He reached out with his staff and shoved the Preacher back, "We are not staying here and you cannot make us stay."

"You dare to shove the Lord's anointed!" screamed the Preacher. Suddenly rage filled his eyes and he raised the iron back. "Then die screaming and know I will have her for myself."

James raised his staff clumsily and managed to intercept the descending bar and to his surprise his staff absorbed the blow easily. With a twist of his wrist he let the bar slide by and it slammed into the floor hard enough to punch a hole into the board. Behind him he heard the outer door slam open and there was a sudden scream, he glanced over his shoulder just long enough to see Cate release an arrow into the darkness outside. A shout of surprise erupted and the would be attackers fell back enough that Cate was able to slam the door and flip down the table in front of it. The moment she turned a resounding crash echoed through the chapel and the door shuddered violently.

"It's not going to hold for long!" Cate shouted.

"Alright," James replied. He looked back just in time to see the Preacher raise his thick iron bar over his head again. This time he jabbed hard and struck him in the solar plexus. With a gasp the man dropped his weapon and grabbed his stomach as the air left his lung with an explosive grunt. A second blow struck him on the head and he folded to the ground silently with his eyes rolled back into his head

"We should go," Cate called. Behind her the door shuddered under a second blow and one of the panels cracked nearly in two. For a moment a furtive face peaked through and stared at them and James thought for a moment that he spotted Billbob's scraggily beard.

"Hold on," James cried. He focused his power and placed a temporary shield in place to hold the doors and windows closed. "That should keep them at bay for a couple of moments. Now let's see what the preacher is keeping in that mine shaft."

"You lead the way," muttered Cate as she eyed the dark hole. She placed another arrow in her bow and followed him through the cabin and into the chapel.

James flipped his hand and a small ball of light appeared, he knew the hand motions were unneeded but he felt better using them. Carefully he positioned it before them and stepped into the wide mouth of the mine. The walls were smooth at first but after about twenty feet the tunnel opened into a wide chamber. Along the walls a dozen cells were cut into the bedrock, each one covered with iron bars set roughly into the stone. Men and women in various states of starvation inhabited seven of the cells. Each of the captives was dark skinned with curly black hair and James shook his head in disgust as he approached the cells and watched the emaciated figures shrink away from him.

"Humanity is nearly wiped out and these idiots revert to slavery," James said in disgust. He reached out with his staff and touched each of the locks willing them to open. As he opened each one he removed the crude iron locks and tossed them into a corner. "Come, I will not harm you." The use of his power cost him little, it was as though his anger acted as a booster focusing the use and cushioning the draining feeling.

Cate smiled encouragingly until a young woman about her age stepped tentatively from the cell, "Come, we will help you escape somehow," Cate encouraged her.

When the young woman realized that no beatings were forthcoming she stumbled from the stone cell and nearly fell into Cate arms.

"James these poor people are so weak they can hardly move," Cate said. There were tears in her eyes as she helped the young lady to a rough bench set along one wall. Two of the men in the cells were so weak that they could not even stand and had to be helped from the cell holding them. Disregarding his usual move towards secrecy James pointed his staff at the floor and began creating a variety of food for the famished people.

"Not too much right away, James," cautioned Cate. Of the seven survivors only three were strong enough to hobble to the food and begin eating so Cate and James took a few moments to carry food and water to each of them. It was nearly ten minutes later when James felt his shield give way under a constant pounding, shouts erupted from the mouth of the tunnel. Cate scrambled for her bow, once she retrieved her weapon she raced to where she would be able to see and shoot down the wide-open tunnel.

"I need some light over here James," Cate cried as she notched an arrow and drew back on her bow.

With a flick of his hand James sent his globe of light racing up the tunnel and anchored it about five feet from the entrance. The first of the town's people that charged down the tunnel was struck in the left shoulder by an arrow and he screamed as he stumbled back away from the deadly darts. Two other men grabbed their wounded compatriot and dragged him away from the entrance and for the time being no other faces appeared.

"Sur, please help us out of here."

James turned and smiled at the woman next to him as she clutched at the sleeve of his robe. Her arms were thin and the skin on her face was stretched so tightly across the bones that she seemed almost skeletal. "I will..." he paused, hoping that she would supply her name.

"My parents called me Keena, sir. God bless you," she said. Tears snaked out of her dark eyes and ran down her face leaving trails in the dried coal dust sticking to all of them.

"Keena, I need you to help me get the others ready to move. I am not sure exactly how we are going to get out yet but we will find a way," James assured her.

"Derek, Star, and Abel over there are strong enough to walk and we will help the others as long as we can." The small amount of food they had eaten already worked wonders on the others and James saw the light slowly returning to their eyes. It was then a grim determination filled him and his fear of directing his power against the people outside evaporated.

"I think you should all step back for a minute. I have an idea about reminding these fools on the surface why their ideas are outdated. Even I know that the Bible said to love your neighbors as yourself." James strode to the tunnel and flicked his hand and sent his light up into the chapel above where he let the ball expand and grow in intensity.

"God has come to us to punish the invaders."

James heard the Preacher crying, apparently he had not struck him hard enough and that was a problem he was going to solve. All eyes were directed at the floating ball of light when James stepped into the chapel. With a snap of his fingers he pointed at the ball and willed forth a brilliant burst of light and sound that resembled a thunderclap. The effect was immediate as the fifty or so men and women inside the chapel collapsed to the floor stunned. Quickly James walked to the front of the chapel and rose into the air until he floated ten feet off the ground. Patently he waited as the effect of his improvised stun grenade wore off.

"Who..."

The Preachers voice trailed off as he looked up to where James floated in the air above the small altar. As others stood slowly their eyes were all drawn to the floating figure robed in white and fairly glowing with barely contained power.

"YOU DARE!" James cried. His voice amplified twenty times. "You dare pretend to be followers of the Bible. God sent fire to cleanse the earth of fools like you and still you dare to hurt your fellow man."

"Lies, they are not like us!" The Preachers shrill cry erupted from where he stood as he shook his fist at James.

"Men like you have always pulled down the rest of humanity with your hatred and stupidity!" James roared. He pointed at the Preacher and willed the man to silence. "No more will you be able to speak to spread your lies. No longer will you be able to eat so that you can feel what you put these poor people through, and last of all no longer will you be able to see so that your final days will be spent in darkness as you made them suffer!" The people gathered in the chapel gasped as he pronounced the curse and a few of women fainted when the Preacher opened his mouth and nothing came forth. The man's mouth opened in what would have been a scream but nothing came out, he reached out his hands as his sight left him and James felt a moment of remorse.

"He is a god!"

"Silence!" roared James. He held up his hand and looked at each of his audience that was still conscious in turn.

"I am not a god! Just a man sent to bring you a message. No longer will you target your fellow humans whether black or white. Your fight is with the ant creatures and those who first attack you. Never more will you take slaves." Every one of the people present nodded their heads and clamored their understanding. "One last thing," James continued as silence once again descended. "You will keep this man until he dies and he will die of starvation." He pointed at the wild-eyed preacher. "Bury him somewhere public as a reminder to all what happens when you do not follow God's words to love your neighbor as yourself. And if I ever hear of you fighting against anyone except in defense of your lives I will return and rain destruction on your heads."

With his last words the people turned on the Preacher, bound his hands and led him from the chapel. When the chapel was empty James allowed himself to float gently to the ground and then he leaned heavily against the rough lectern. Despite the rage he still felt over the acts of these people he had not expended this amount of power in a while and he had forgotten how tired it made him feel.

18 Keena

That night James led the seven rescued slaves from a silent town with the entire population of the town watching. As they neared the main gate Billbob stepped out from the twenty or so men crowded around the gate and nervously rolled his hat in his hands.

"Billbob," James said coldly. Inwardly he was thankful for the pause, with a hard glare he leaned on his staff in a pose he hoped was intimidating and waited for the man to speak

"Sir, I know we did wrong but we wanted to send you out with some food and things," Billbob said. He motioned the men forward and slowly each man stepped forward and set a basket of goods on the ground. Some laid down blankets, some brought fresh changes of clothes, and some offered crude but effective weapons. When they had laid it all at James's feet they turned and shuffled away trying to move quickly but not make it obvious that they wanted away from him.

"Nice work, James," smiled Cate. She picked through the clothes and found some that would fit Keena. Working as quickly as they could James and Cate found clothes that fit each of the former slaves and then went to work making packs filled with food and a blanket for each of the slaves. In the end James and Cate ended up carrying most of what they packed, the former slaves were simply too weak to help much.

It was near midnight, James thought, when they stopped and made camp in the protective circle of pine trees growing on top of a nearby hilltop. The few torches and lights in the village were still glowing on the distant horizon but even with food in their stomachs the rescued men and women could go no further. Even more he was beginning to stumble and the last thing he needed was to collapse before the people around him. When James called a halt to the march most of them fell to the ground, pulled their blankets up, and fell asleep.

"What have I got myself into?" James muttered. He stood on the edge of their small camp and looked over the group. "I have tried to right every wrong that I have found and what has it gained me. Seven more mouths to feed and ones that cannot even defend themselves until they regain their strength."

"You're a good man James."

He jumped at the voice behind him but it was a voice that he knew so he turned and smiled at Cate. "I didn't hear you coming." James laughed quietly as he looked at her. "I am just whining. I wouldn't change anything I have done."

"That is good because the world needs more like you in it," Cate said quietly. She stepped close to him and gazed up into his eyes for a long moment, almost imperceptibly she leaned forward until her lips brushed against his cheek. "I have only known you for a short time but you're a good man, James. After we have visited your family home and you have laid your demons to rest I will be waiting for you." With those words she turned and walked to where Keena was sleeping. There she rolled into her blanket and closed her eyes.

"I will wake you for your watch," James said. All she did in response was nod lightly and then her breathing evened and silence descended on the camp.

James brushed his hand lightly across his cheek where her lips touched him as he sat down on a nearby log. Quickly he found his mind wandering the rooms of his house in St Cloud. He could hear in his mind the laughter of his son as he played in the yard outside, and the sounds of his wife playing the piano in the front room. The wood floors amplified the sound and brought it to many of the rooms in the house even above the rumble of the nearby Mississippi River. In his nostrils he smelled the freshly cut grass in the backyard mixed with the perfume his wife wore. As the night wore on his memories kept him company and helped him stay awake as he relived a hundred different events, smells, and sounds. Slowly a single tear rolled down his cheek, but moments later it was followed by more and soon the trickle became a flood. He suffered through the tears silently knowing that in morning he would have to strong again.

James woke Cate after what he assumed was four hours and then he rolled himself into an empty blanket and drifted off to sleep. This night his dreams were quiet and filled with wonderful memories.

Cate prowled the perimeter of the campsite for almost two hours listening and watching for any sign of pursuit. The armored cloth that James had made her fit like a second skin but was so soft that it moved against her skin like a scrap of silk that her father showed her a few years ago. Her feelings for James were powerful but she was unsure why they were so powerful. From the moment she looked up from the muddy banks of the Old Miss River she had been drawn to him. Never before had any man affected her so, before the attack on her village she had courted with three different men but turned down each for various reasons.

"Why now?" she pondered out loud.

"What is it, miss?"

Cate jumped at the voice that spoke directly behind her, so wrapped up in her private thoughts she had ignored her watchfulness. She turned and looked to where Keena propped her upper body up on her left elbow and looked through the last few minutes of darkness that night laid on them. The black woman's skin was well hidden against the night but her eyes shone brightly in the last rays of the moon.

"I was just thinking out loud..." Cate said. She crossed the camp and squatted down on her haunches with her bow across her knees. From there she could still see most of the shallow valley laid out before them. "I have been around men most of my life but never have I had feelings about someone that so confuse me. I feel drawn to him as a man but it is more than that. You have seen his power and how he uses it. Think of it, he could have carved himself an empire out of the lands around him. Yet he is traveling to where he believes his family died and he has stopped to help when he could have easily passed each of us by."

Keena nodded, "I felt it too. He is a good man and handsome but I want what he has. I am sick of being hunted because of the color of my skin. Derek and Able grew up with me in a hidden village near the great Atlantic Ocean to the east. Without warning one day, we were attacked by raiders from the sea and twenty survived to flee. Three died to disease as we traveled and then ten more were worked to death by the Preacher and the people of Kentuck."

Cate nodded, "My people were attacked by a group called the Cajune."

"I want to be able to help my people find a place of safety, but there is something even more powerful pushing me towards him. The moment I saw him I knew I would follow him no matter what he says until I can find a way to the power he has." Keena stopped as she struggled with the words for a moment. "And somehow I know that I would use the power as he does. At least I believe that I would."

Cate nodded as she put her hand out and rested in comfortingly on Keena's arm. She could not explain it but she felt a connection with her in a way that only sisters normally did. The type of connection that she thought they would someday know what each other was thinking, "I never thought I would find a sister so far from home."

Keena smiled her agreement and hugged Cate lightly, "Sisters."

Cate stood and walked to where Able and Star were beginning to stir in their blankets, of the two, Star was stronger so she woke the older woman and together with Keena they began preparing what food they possessed. The village of Kentuck sent them out with many of the basics including several battered pans and a small pot. Working quickly Star constructed a sturdy tripod out of thick branches stripped of their leaves. From the top of the tripod she hung a battered but solid pot after filling it with water. Keena started a small fire under the pot and found a package that was filled with some type of mashed oats. One of the villages sent a small container of honey and so they breakfasted that morning on hot porridge and honey before packing up their camp.

James was silent for much of the morning and when he finally turned to speak he seemed to understand that something had taken place during the night between Keena and Cate.

"Where will you go?" James asked Star.

She shrugged, "Back to the coast I think. I don't know where we can be safe but there were rumors of a large group of our people to the north along the coast. It will take us at least twenty days of walking to get back to the coast. Even if we manage to walk that far I do not know if we can fend off wild animals let alone people like those behind us."

"Wait a minute?" James muttered. "Twenty days to the east coast?" that can't be possible. It should be hundreds of miles to the east coast."

"Not any more, when the sky burned the lands changed, there is a wide channel of seawater. However, my father told me that he once sailed to a large island several dozen miles across the water."

James shook his head as he thought about how much more of the lands that he knew had changed. If much of the east coast was now separated from the main land what else could have happened. Was Minnesota even close to what had been when he flew out of the Humphrey Terminal in Minneapolis? When he arrived would he find a desert or a swamp or even a new mountain range raised by the massive impacts?

"And what of you Keena?" James questioned.

"Cate and I talked and I have decided to join her and travel with you."

"Don't I get a choice in this?" asked James with a smile dancing around his lips. He did feel a twinge of irritation at the thought of another person slowing down his journey north but he did somehow know that Keena and Cate were wrapped up in his own future.

"This is bigger than us, James Kaning and I think you know that," Cate said quietly. Standing next to her Keena nodded her agreement; both of their faces were set with a resolve that startled James so much that for a moment he thought of fleeing.

They separated ways when the sun was near its height, James, Cate, and Keena started north on foot. James turned the sailboat over to the six survivors along with all the supplies carefully horded on the trip north.

"You should be able to sail back down the Mississippi river all the way to the coast. The current and wind will make the trip go quickly, then just swing east and follow the coast. You can fish to supplement your food supply but be careful where you put ashore." James kept a running commentary until they were waving from almost two hundred yards downriver. They watched for nearly ten minutes until the bobbing sailboat appeared only as a speck in the distance.

"Well, north it is," James muttered. He shouldered the remaining supplies stuffed into his leather pack and shifted it until he found a comfortable spot for it. Cate and Keena split the remaining supplies between them and followed him as he started north. On a whim James broke off a thick willow branch as they left the riverbank and began working the wood. It was late evening when he finished with the bow and quiver. Somehow it was easier to work slowly and with existing materials then to just create something from thin air. Easier and it felt more natural to him.

"Can you shoot a bow?" James asked as he passed Keena the weapon.

"Not really but I think Cate can show me the basics," Keena replied. She swung the belt holding the quiver around her waist just like Cate wore hers and then tested the draw on the powerful bow.

James nodded as his mind drifted on to other problems. The land around them was rugged but as his eyes searched the low lands below them he noticed a feature that made his heart beat a bit faster.

"There, we need to get off these ridges and get down to the flat area," James said. He pointed down to where a wide flat strip of land stretched out as far as the eye can see.

"Why is that?" Cate asked.

"See the remains of that sign over there?" James asked. He pointed to where the four massive iron posts still rose up from the ground, fallen on the dirt behind the posts he could read the words that still held the color of their original paints even after nearly one hundred years.

"What does it say?" Keena asked.

"It says Chicago, Illinois four hundred and twenty miles." As James read the words his heart sighed, it would take the rest of the summer to walk to Minnesota. Even if they covered fifteen miles a day it would take at least thirty days just reach Chicago. Then it would take at least, another thirty or forty days to travel across Wisconsin to Minnesota.

"Can you read Keena?" James asked suddenly. He turned and looked at her with sympathetic eyes.

"No, my father always said it was a waste of time."

"Well, we will have to change that, Cate can help you start learning the basics and then we can work on your math skills also."

"Why would I need to learn that?" Keena asked. They were walking down a rocky slope covered only with a light sprinkling of trees and underbrush. They were half way down the slope and James stopped for a moment and looked back at her. "Keena, I know that someday you want be like me with access to a power that has not been seen on this world in many thousands of years. Never forget that if you gain it without practical knowledge you will fail in the end."

Keena nodded, seeing that this was a serious matter to James and therefore she would apply herself to learning to reading and write and whatever else he deemed necessary.

James turned back to the trail leading down to what he assumed was the remains of Interstate sixty-five running from Mobile Alabama to Gary Indiana. It took nearly an hour to cover the remaining distance and for James to confirm his suspicion. At first he found several mile markers that survived the onslaught of time and then a faded sign that proudly proclaimed the number sixty inside the shield shaped emblem. A thick layer of grass now largely hid the remains of the pavement but when he paused to clear away some of the topsoil he still found remains of the thick tar.

"What is that?" Cate asked suddenly. She pointed to where a long metal box lay on its side off the side of the remains of the road.

"Semi truck," James said. He pointed to where the rusted remains of the big truck were still attached to the trailer. "Shall we see what it was carrying?" He walked the last hundred yards to where the trailer lay and paused at the gaping hole drilled in the side of the steel box. The trailer must have taken a direct hit from a small meteor because the far side was completely obliterated and much of what the truck had carried had been destroyed. The rest was rotted and rusted beyond recognition. James circled the truck once tapping on the metal but much of it was rusted so badly that little remained that was sturdy; the one part of the truck that had survived well enough was the barrel shaped tank of diesel. Carefully James worked the cap off and sniffed the opening, "Still smells like diesel."

They continued north along interstate 60 for nearly eight days before James saw the first signs of life other then animals. Deer seemed to have survived and flourished in the post apocalyptic events of the past. Massive herds of white tails raised their heads and stared warily at them as they passed but many lowered their heads and continued grazing. Here and there were signs of predators but they were few and far in between.

They entered a flat area and James assumed that it was beginning of the plains of central Ohio, it was hard to tell but he thought they had made good time. It was confirmed when he spotted a surviving road sign and marked the fact that they were now three hundred and twelve miles left to Chicago.

"James, someone is coming," Cate said. She motioned to the east where a plume of smoke or dust marked the approach of something large.

"Let's move towards that outcropping of rocks." James pointed to the north were the highway bed turned west slowly and cut through a wide hill. At some point in the past the cliff overlooking the highway had collapsed and left a pile of rubble and in the process provided them with a perfect hiding place. The two women nodded and began jogging quickly towards the tumble of stones. James followed them, as he ran he glanced over his shoulder and marked the approach of what seemed to be a large group of horses and riders.

They reached the fifty-foot high cliff and immediately took refuge among the jumble of stones and massive boulders. James puffed some as he crouched to watch the approach of the riders. Now he could see individual riders and he counted nearly thirty men racing towards their hiding place.

"Do they look friendly?" Keena asked. Both she and Cate had notched arrows and held their bows ready to fire at a moment's notice.

"I will go out and see what they want," James said. Carefully he constructed a thick shield around himself and then arranged a bit of camouflage for the women. When he felt he was ready he squared his shoulders and stepped out from between the thick boulders. The riders spotted him immediately and swept out in a wide half moon to surround him and cut off all chance of escape. Most of the riders wielded a lance like weapon with a sharpened steel head that was nearly a foot long. He also spotted a few crude short bows among the riders and he was careful to keep his hands open in what he considered a non-threatening posture.

"Greetings," James called. He smiled widely as he watched a single tall rider nudge his mount forward. Thankfully his hood was already back and his view of the surrounding riders was unobstructed and so his heart beat a bit faster when he saw several of the riders prepare their bows. "We come in peace," James tried again to establish contact.

"Why have you come to our lands?"

James sighed in relief; he knew his shield would stand up to a few of the arrows but considering he had never tried them in an outright battle he didn't feel like testing them now.

"We are just traveling to the lands to the north, a state once known as Minnesota. If we have trespassed on your lands we did not realize."

"Where did you come from?"

The same tall rider demanded, he seemed to be gauging James's replies and waited with his weapons ready.

"I came from very far down river, all the way to the Caribbean Sea, my companions joined me as I sailed up river. About nine days ago we rescued a group of people held captive in town up in the mountains and I sent them south in my own boat. We continued north on foot," James explained. He noticed that some of the riders seemed to have dismissed him as a threat and they now watched the lands around them closely. Most of the men wore faded jeans and a few, he noticed, had leather boots that must have survived the fires he assumed would have raged through most major cities after the meteor strikes. Many were bare-chested but a few wore rough leather vests that appeared to have been made some time after the industrial age.

"Why are you going north?"

James sensed that this was the last question so he answered, "I wish to visit the place where I believe my wife and son died. After that I don't know what I will do." The answers seemed to satisfy and the tall rider turned and motioned to the men around him.

"Go scout the plains to the west, we know the creatures are moving again. If you find them send someone back for me, I want to see them die with my own eyes." He slipped from his saddle and approached James offering his hand in greeting. "My name is John McMintire and these lands belong to my family as do the herds of cattle that roam on them."

James shook his hand firmly and then motioned with his hand to Cate and Keena, "You can come out now." John's eyes widened visibly when he saw the two women appear from what seemed thin air holding bows that dwarfed his own rider's weapons.

"You spoke true when you said you had companions although I saw no one here a moment ago," John said warily.

"We mean no harm," James assured. "I heard you speak of creatures a minute ago, they don't look like giant ant with pincers do they?"

"Yes, did you see them?" John asked. He fingered his long knives hanging from his belt and a glint appeared in his eyes.

"Not this particular group but I saw them far to the south along the coasts," James admitted. "I saw many of them in towering clay and mud mounds dried hard by the sun."

"And we heard of them scouting a town to the south in the mountains," Cate said. She stood near James right side and stared wide eyed at the bay stallion that stood cropping grass just behind John. She had not seen such a magnificent animal in her life time and she wanted so badly to ride the beast.

"Yes, they slaughtered hundreds of our cattle and a few of our ranch hands. When I arrived with more men they ran and we have hunted them now for two days. Yesterday we caught three of them and killed them at the loss of four of my own riders."

James nodded as he listened, "Appears that those creatures are scouting new lands I would say."

"Well, they will not find here," John muttered. Suddenly a piercing whistle echoed from the west and John turned and leaped into the saddle. "They cornered them!" he shouted. "I will return when this business is done." With that he pulled his mounts head around and raced away to where a cloud of dust gathered around a scurry of small figures.

"We should see if we can go help," James said.

"I am game," Keena smiled.

Cate nodded and pulled an arrow from her quiver as they turned and began jogging towards the distant battle.

James watched the battle through eyes that were enhanced for distance as he jogged towards them. At first it seemed that they would never arrive in time but then several of the creatures broke from the encircling riders and ran towards them almost as fast as a horse can gallop.

"Better get your bow ready," James said as he altered his course to put himself in line with a small rise. When they arrived at the hill the ant like monsters were one hundred yards away and closing fast. Cate loosed her first arrow at fifty yards and smiled grimly as the razor sharp shaft flew true and struck the creature in the middle of his armored thorax. The shaft stuck tight in this thick armor but didn't seem to slow it much.

"Crap!" growled Cate as she pulled another shaft free of her quiver. Next to her Keena loosed her first arrow but it flew wide and disappeared into the grass. Cate next shaft took flight when the creature was thirty yards out and this time James gave the arrow a bit of a boost. He willed the arrow to strike true and it took the monster directly in its head. This time the creature stumbled to a halt and then slowly sank to the ground as its brain finally shut down and took the massive body with it.

"Wahoo!" Cate cried out but then her voice stuck in her throat as a second monstrous creature skirted the first and charged them.

Keena cried out and loosed her second arrow as panic set in and the shaft flew wide to the right but suddenly the arrow seemed to pause in flight then did an amazing thing. As the dark skinned archer watched the arrow turned in a long lazy arc and struck the second giant ant directly in the back of the chest. This time the effect was more pronounced then hitting it from the front. The creature stumbled and slumped to the ground. By this time the remaining hands had finished their battle and were racing towards them.

James took a quick count as they approached and noted the band of riders once again seemed a bit smaller. On the plains half a mile away the remainder of the ant creatures scouting party lay on the ground hacked down by the long pole arms.

"Are you alright?" John asked. Again he swung down approached them but this time a smile lit his face.

"Yes," James replied. "Thanks to the lethal aim of my friends here." He opted to give the credit to Cate and Keena rather than take it for himself. In the long run it may be worth more to have the two women looked at as deadly warriors able to strike fear into the hearts of any who would stand against them.

A look of respect leaped into John's eyes almost immediately and he smiled graciously to the pair of archers. "You should return to our homestead. My father would enjoy meeting you and swapping stories."

"Is it far?" James asked. The trip home was still foremost in his mind and he was anxious over any interruption that slowed his northern progress.

"Not more than a few hours ride," John said. "And I can assure you that father will be grateful enough to meet other survivors that I can persuade him to part with mounts for your journey."

James brightened considerably at that and nodded his agreement. With horses at their disposal the trip back to the land of lakes would be much faster. To that end he climbed aboard the offered mount and followed the band of riders back to the east. Only one of the dead rider's horses had survived the attack and so James found himself riding double with Cate, while Keena mounted behind John for the ride. She wrapped her arms around him tightly and held him so close that James felt the fear and trembling in her limbs.

"Don't worry Cate, I don't think John would have given us this mount if there were a chance of us falling off," James said over his shoulder.

She grunted something under her breath and continued to hold him as tightly as she could, whimpering each time the band urged their mounts to faster speeds. She wanted to ride but would have preferred a nice slow walk in a paddock first.

It took nearly three hours of riding to reach the ranch operated by John's father and his extended family. James was amazed to find that far from being a medieval collection of buildings the family had constructed a solid and well built collection of dwellings that closed in on all four sides to form an easily defended fort. The outer walls of the buildings that faced the plains were over a foot thick. John proclaimed they had withstood every attack directed against them thus far. The complex of buildings included a rough smithy, a windmill that powered an old fashion pump to bring fresh water out of a deep well, and last of all a set of ponds built into the top and bottom of a steep hill. James watched the water wheel spin slowly and turn a pair of shafts that reached to a pair of outbuildings just outside the main complex.

"Where did you get all the lumber?" James asked.

"There is an old growth forest that survived the devastation brought by the meteors just north of here. We cut what we need and then drag the logs back," John replied.

"Your father remembers what happened?" asked James in surprise.

"Yes," John nodded as he directed his men back towards the safety of the thick walls. "His father was a rancher who got lucky and survived the attack. He recorded what happened in a book and passed it on to my father, in turn, my father had me read it when I turned eighteen. Grandpa was a mechanical engineer and he included many drawings of things he thought would be useful. It is his drawings that helped us build the mill and the holding ponds to power it."

"Amazing," James muttered. "I would very much like to see that book."

"That might be arranged." John seemed a bit evasive when James continued to press about the mechanical drawings so he allowed the subject to drop. With a loud whoop John led his ranch hands down the hill and thundered across the last half mile of plains separating them from the sprawling collection of buildings.

James turned slightly in the saddle so he could see Cate's face and then spoke, "What do you think of our new friend?"

"Seems friendly and fair but he is definitely hiding something about the book," Cate responded. She tightened her grip as the horse under them pranced about wanting to follow the rest of the mounts.

James nodded. He let the horse have its head but held it back from going into a gallop. In his mind he mulled over the events of the past weeks with an analytical approach trying to fathom what would wait for him in the land of lakes. So far he knew the people who survived in the swamps of the deep south were cannibalistic and would have to be avoided at all costs on later trips, the villages inhabiting the remains of the Cumberland mountains were tending towards their segregated past but that might be changed given time, and for now the plains folk seemed to be fair minded if secretive. He needed a book to write his observations in and that was something he would have to turn his mind to later.

"Book!" James muttered suddenly. "I should start some type of record."

"What?" asked Cate?

"Nothing, just thinking out loud," James called over his shoulder.

"Now you're not being completely honest with me," Cate retorted. She jabbed him in the side playfully but also as a reminder not to complain if others kept their secrets close at hand.

"I promise I will explain it to you tonight, when I can talk to you and Keena privately." James turned his attention back to the trail and the waiting wooden gate. They trotted through the portal and reined to a halt in the middle of the wide yard. An elderly man waited for them, standing beside him was John and the common ancestry was immediately apparent.

19 Riders of the Range

"Welcome to our home."

"Thank you," James replied. He reached back and helped Cate swing down off the back of the horse they were riding and then he carefully swung his own legs off the brown mare. Already his muscles were a bit stiff and he noticed that Keena and Cate seemed to be having the same problem he was walking.

"My son tells me that you killed two of the Gyants by yourselves."

"Both of the ladies are excellent shots with their bows," James replied calmly. He accepted the proffered hand with a nod and returned the handshake firmly, the elder man's hand was covered in calluses and his skin was a leathery brown from constant exposure to the sun and elements.

"I am John McMintire Sr. the boy tells me that you remember the day the sky burned?" John Sr. asked curiously.

James shrugged ambiguously, "It is something I would like to discuss with you in private if that is possible. With the exception of John, Cate, and Keena of course."

John Sr. nodded and spoke to his men, "Take care of the mounts and then get yourselves some food."

After he dismissed his ranch hands he motioned for James and the others to follow him. His riders set to work immediately and when James looked back they were hauling the saddles into one of the low ceiling buildings while others rubbed the mounts down with stiff hand brushes. James watched everything as they walked towards the sprawling single story ranch house, and he realized as he looked about how much the dwelling resembled an nineteenth century ranch. A wide porch with log railings fronted each building offering a place of relief from the heat of the midday sun. A series of small bridges crossed a small stream of water directed from the mill ponds to a wide garden sheltered between the ranch house and another long building.

Still despite the warmth of the mid day sun and the good breeze blowing from the east the grass was green. "Does it rain here often?" James asked.

"About twice a week," John answered. "According to grandpa before he died the rains never came that often before the meteors came."

"Boy!" John sr. barked. "Hold your tongue."

"It's alright Mr. McMintire," James said softly. "I know more about that event then probably any man alive today. Well except for one other." He thought about Alan suddenly and wondered what the other archeologist was doing, but that was a line of reasoning he forced from his mind quickly. With the darkness that he saw in Alan's behavior even before that day almost a century ago he shuddered to think what the other man was capable of with his new powers.

"Still, better discuss this where the chance of being over heard is less. Many of the ranch hands here have never known any life other than ours and they and their families really have no interest in the old times. They are better left as they are, the stuff of past years brought great evil to the world. We have been given a chance to start over and the people here are starting over."

James furrowed his brow trying to understand the elder man's line of reasoning but failing miserably.

"My son still thinks that there are things from the old world that we could use to make our lives easier. He thinks I should send scouting parties out searching for artifacts so that we can unlock the secrets of our ancestors," John Sr. muttered. The elder man fell silent then as they mounted the steps to the ranch house. It was a modest affair and the size of the building was deceptive when James realized that five different families were housed in wings of the overall building.

They walked down the wooden floors until they reached a small study and elder man opened the door wide for them. The room was crowded with all five present but James stood with his back to the wall while John stood just behind his father with a frown painted across his face. It was plain that he and his father disagreed about the direction the small community was taking but James decided to leave for now.

"Of all the places we have visited your ranch is impressive," James started.

"Yes, right now we run about two thousand head of cattle," John boasted with a broad smile. "We plant and mill our own grain, grow our own vegetables make our own leather, and we are even raising a few milk cows traded from…"

"Hsst!"

John fell silent as his father rounded on him, "Outsiders do not need to know all of our business dealings. We do not even know these people yet!"

James waited until he was done talking and then stepped forward towards the small wooden desk until he looked down at the two ranchers. "Understand something, I have been alive for longer than both of you can imagine and if I had wanted to harm either of you I would have down it by now." James's voice rose until it resembled caged thunder. "If the human race is to survive in this new order that has arisen we will have to learn to set aside petty differences and trust those who offer the hand of friendship." As he spoke the last words he let his presence fill the room until he fairly towered over the two men.

"How…" John Sr. muttered. He fell back in his seat with his eyes wide with fear. With a trembling hand he made the sign of the cross hoping to ward off the evil that he believed now faced them.

"I said, I come in peace," James repeated. He let the illusion drop away and offered them his warmest smile. "There are others who will deserve to be questioned but I am not one of them. Give me a chance and I will help you turn your people into a dominant presence across the Great Plains."

"Better believe him," Cate said suddenly breaking the terrified silence that filled the room. "I have been with him for some weeks now and every time we see someone in need of help James rushes to the rescue even when it would be much easier for him to turn a blind eye." She smiled up at him with a crooked but affectionate smile and patted his arm.

Keena added an emphatic nod that made her dark curls bounce wildly as they framed the fine lines of her face. James was suddenly struck at how much she reminded him of the generation of actress that filled the beginning part of the twenty-first century.

"I believe," John stammered. "I believe."

His father simply nodded as the fear slowly faded from his eyes and a look of hope erupted. "Can you find my son?" he whispered.

"What?" James asked as the question took him by surprise.

John grimaced and laid a hand on his father's shoulder, "My youngest brother was taken by the Gyants nearly four months ago. We do have contacts with other groups living in the area and all of them have similar stories. Children taken in midnight raids, they are taken by people and creatures working in concert."

"I can see why you would be suspicious of strangers," James muttered.

"Yes, well, there is another part of the story," John said. He glanced about almost fearfully despite the fact that he was standing safely inside his own home. "It is said the kidnappers move in shadows, they come in through locked doors, past scores of watchers, and strike where people think they are safest."

Cate and Keena looked at other as the shock showed in their eyes, the idea that despite the strong walls around them there were creatures that could still strike at any time would shake anyone to the core. Both of them fingered their bows wondering if they would need to use the weapons anytime soon.

James leaned carefully on the back of the chair where Keena sat and eyed John, "Sounds like magic, doesn't it."

"Yes," John agreed.

"I only know one other man who is able to use magic," John muttered. "I think it is time I told my story in full. If magic is involved then we may have bigger problems than anyone can understand."

James started his story with the trip to Central America and the movements of the massive hurricane that made their guides flee. He told them of the temple and the amazing detail of the building itself and the feat of engineering performed by those who built it. When he described the tunnel leading into the earth and the amazing rainbow of lights that lit the shaft it brought gasps of awe. Finally his words took them into the central chamber and then showed them the device that changed both Alan and himself. Past that, he laid out the choice that he faced when he accepted the power. Even more amazing was the gap of time he spent sleeping as his body changed.

"You slept for nearly a hundred years?" question John.

"Yes, at least as near as I can figure the time. I watched the sky burn with hundreds and even thousands of meteors race across the sky. Both of us awoke every so often to eat vast amounts of food and spend some time moving around but the rest of the time it seemed like we were held outside the flow of time. I cannot explain how or why it happened."

" you have rested a hundred years?" Cate asked suddenly. It was as though his words had stomped the wind from her sails.

"That is how long it has been for me, Cate," James said apologetically. "I would have told you all the details of what happened to me before I took you anywhere near the machine.

She looked him uncertainly, not sure if she was angry to not have known that fact or simply stunned that she would be alive for that long. Cate glanced at Keena but the other woman simply shrugged, marking her acceptance of the idea.

"I would do anything to help my people, even if it takes me a hundred years. That is a drop in the vast well of time," Keena said proudly. Her chin was thrust out and her jaw set in a firm line that spoke of her determination

"I wonder if Alan found a group of followers and then managed to figure out how to adapt their physical bodies through his power," James muttered. His mind reeled as he considered the possibilities and things that should or should not be done. He had never really considered that his power could be used to alter the physical beings of people or animals and now he was sickened by the thought of what could happen.

"I don't think that is something that my understanding of this magic would allow me to do. Or maybe I should say the barriers of my choices would not allow me," James said slowly. "But I know that Alan chose the darker side of the magic and it very well may be in his sphere of power. If that is so, then we will need to find a way to counter what he is doing and if possible, rescue those taken captive."

"I think it is time for a meeting of the families."

All eyes turned suddenly to John Sr. as he spoke after his long silence. There was a light in his eyes that John had not seen in many months.

"Dad, do you think they will come?"

"We must try," John Sr. said. "Call for volunteers to carry messages to the others. We will host the meeting on our lands and all are invited."

"And if they turn us down?" John asked.

"No one will turn down the chance to retrieve the missing..."

James had been staring at the ceiling as he considered the events happening around him when he heard the elder plainsman's voice fade off. He glanced to where John and his father stood at the small desk and his eyes immediately found the shadow in the corner and he felt the presence of something standing in the shadow.

"Light!" James thundered. Immediately his globe of light erupted and darted into the corner burning with the power of a miniature sun. On a whim he sent three more globes into the other four corners and banished every bit of shadow from the small room.

"What is it?" Cate asked. Her voice trembled as she looked at the huddled creature on the floor. It was vaguely human shaped but bent and twisted beyond belief. Its skin and body seemed to be trying to shift back into the shadows that no longer existed in the room.

"The light seems to be hurting it," Keena said. Of those present she had the presence of mind to grab an arrow, notch it, and draw her bow. She kept the razor sharp arrow pointed at the creature watching intently for any sign of an attempt to flee.

"I can see Alan's fingers all over it," James muttered. The moment he had spotted the creature he had banished the shadows and then used his inner senses to examine it. What he found turned his stomach so wildly that he nearly emptied it on the floor before him. He could see the areas of the man that Alan had changed and what's more he could feel the binding that the other man had placed on the twisted human's spirit.

"Can you change it back?" John asked suddenly.

"I wouldn't know where to start," James replied. "But it may offer us a clue to what we face."

James stood and walked to where the creature huddled, carefully he let his senses flow over the creatures mind until he found what was left of his memory. Without even knowing how, he began seeing through the monsters eyes as it slipped by the watchers on the walls outside avoiding any contact with the light cast by dozens of torches. He pressed back further picking up glimpses of a journey that brought it down from the north seeking targets for his masters. James glimpsed the outskirts of Chicago before the creature suddenly cried out and leaped at him.

"Look out!" Cate cried.

John scrambled to draw his belt knife and move into striking distance, pushing in front of his father to protect the elder man.

Keena calmly sight down her arrow and released the shaft in the midst of the chaos. Her aim was true and the arrow pinioned the shadow man to the wall next to the door. As she drew her second arrow it seemed like time slowed around her and she sunk the next arrow through the creatures shoulder as it struggled to remove the first, then chaos erupted around her.

Moment's later order once again descended on the tight confines of the room and James stared at the shadow man as it struggled against the two arrows holding it tightly to the wall.

"We need to go north to old Chicago," James said. He saw with interest that the shadow still bled red blood and it dripped slowly to the floor as the struggles became weaker and weaker.

"The City on the Lake is a bastion of filth." John spat on the floor as he spoke. "They kill anyone who tries to enter their territory."

"That is where the creature has its base. It stands to reason that if it is coming from the city then maybe Alan is there, but somehow I don't think he is." James muttered. For some unknown reason he had the feeling the other man was further away. He got the impression from the shadow that it had only recently arrived in the area from somewhere else.

The spent the rest of the night dozing lightly with dozens of torches burning to banish the shadows and when morning came James found that he was still tired. He yawned loudly as they gathered to the breakfast table and ate a healthy breakfast of eggs and flapjacks. Somewhere the ranchers had found maple trees and the thick syrup tasted like heaven to him.

"This is great," James muttered around a big mouthful. He looked up to see both Cate and Keena smiling at him and once again he had this sudden urge to run like hell. Instead he smiled sheepishly and then turned back to his plate. The ranchers used glazed pottery cookware and even managed to construct pipes to bring fresh water into the various buildings around the spread.

"Clay pipes," John said when James asked him. "One of the things my great grandfather's book talked about."

James nodded.

When the meal was done they walked out onto the porch and watched as nearly thirty ranch hands and various members of John's family saddled horses and hitched teams to wagons that reminded James of old covered wagons that he had seen in the movies. Crates of supplies were stacked in each of the wagons and spare weapons bundled to the side within easy reach of the outriders.

"Are any staying?"

"Only a few to watch for fires and ride to warn us if the Gyants return."

"Where is the meeting place?" James asked. Carefully he swung his leg over the waiting mare and settled into the saddle. Despite the nights rest his legs and butt still ached and the thought of a long ride made him very uncomfortable.

"North about five days ride," John said. He motioned to the north casually and his point took in what seemed to be a thousand miles of prairie.

20 City by the Lake

Five days later James was thankful to see an outrider race back to them waving and smiling broadly. Twenty minutes later he entered the gather place and James was stunned to find nearly seven hundred of the range men gathered with their families and even much of their live stock.

"The cattle are our lives," John explained with James pointed out the vast herds of longhorns. "If we lose our ranches we can rebuild but if we lose our cattle we have no source of food and the thousand other things we gain from them."

"I see," James said. He never considered cattle beyond where his next hamburger was coming from but when they were your life's blood they became much more important.

That night they came together for a meeting around a massive camp fire and the reasons for the gathering were laid out for all to see.

"This is why we are here," John called out for the gathered men and women to hear. With a motion of his hand four of his men pulled the wooden pins holding the back of a covered wagon closed and then disappeared into the wagon. Moments later the oversized body of grotesquely mutated ant tumbled between the canvas covers followed moments later by the arrow pierced body of the shadow man.

"The Gyant was killed almost seven days ago on the south western edge of our grazing range and the shadow man was killed with the help of our new friend six days ago." Gasps filled the area around the fire as the range riders crowded close to examine the shadow man. The Gyants they had seen before, and indeed, many had fought them in running battles across the plains but for someone to stop a shadow man was almost an unheard of event.

When the initial outburst had faded a bit, John called for silence and then continued. "All of us have lost family to the creatures, most of them children, kidnapped at night. Taken from their beds and the safety of their homes with no warning and up until now we have been powerless to stop them. But six days ago James Kaning banished the shadows from the father's office ,and his lady friend brought the creature down with two well placed arrows."

At this point a rousing cheer erupted and Keena suddenly found herself the center of attention which made her blush fiercely. Smiling and shaking hands, she endured the praise until nearly everyone present had shaken her hand.

"Even more, James was able to see through the creatures eyes during the last moments of its life. We think we know where the shadow men have taken our children and by god it is time for the little ones to come home."

This declaration brought a thunderous roar as more and more of the plainsmen drifted closer to hear the words of the gathering. It was some time until John was able to restore enough order to continue. After nearly thirty minutes James decided that if he didn't do something the plains men would continue to talk until the moon was high. Not wanting to scare anyone he finally summoned his shining ball of light and let it float up into the air above his head. Almost immediately a hush came across the gathering as all eyes turned to watch the light. Casually James let it fall back to his hand, then, with a flick of his wrist, he sent it bobbing around the fire. Finally, with a tiny popping sound, he willed it away and turned back to John.

"Please, good people, we need to concentrate on planning and listen to John. I cannot wait for days while you talk about doing this. We need to move quickly; for all we know the shadow men could be moving your children even now." The thought of them losing their chance to rescue the lost children sobered everyone immediately and John was allowed to continue uninterrupted.

"It is my thought that we all contribute three or four men to a rescue force. Understand though, that James and myself will direct this force only. Once the children are safely in our hands we will return to the gathering."

There were many nods of consent and only a few shouted suggestions until a grizzled old man asked in a rough voice that reminded James of two pieces of sandpaper rubbing together.

"Where be the children?"

"James believes that the shadow men were using the City by the Lake for their base," John replied.

James looked around in surprise as silence filled the air until it was an almost oppressive feeling. Many of the men made the sign of the cross and even more faces went pale at the mention of old Chicago.

"Then the children be lost to us," the old man concluded. "And if you go there you will be lost to us too."

"And what would you have us do!" John nearly shouted. "Turn tail and run until we are found again. How many will be lost each time before we decide to run again and who will volunteer their children to be sacrificed."

James took stock of the feelings around him this time using his inner senses; all around him he felt despair and frustration. Under those feelings though, he also felt a streak of determination in many and keeping this in mind he raised his hands for silence.

"Good people, the group of men that accompanies us does not need to be large. What we must do we will do by stealth not by brute force. If old Chicago has gotten as bad as everyone tells me it has, then an attack by an armed force of cavalry would do us little good. A small group led by myself will enter the city and find the children, once we have accomplished our mission I assure you we will find a way to meet the waiting group. Even if I must burn the city to the ground a third time." James let his voice grow bigger and more forceful as he spoke until it nearly thundered across the plains. When he was finished he met the eyes of as many of the people around him as he could and spoke softly but oddly enough that everyone around him heard. "And trust me I can burn that city to the ground if I so choose."

Nodding to John, James turned and motioned to Cate and Keena, together they left the range riders to work out the details of the mounted force and went in search of food.

"Do you really mean it?" Cate asked suddenly as they sat on a long log pulled up near a small cooking fire. "Could you burn the city to the ground if you wanted?"

"Yes," James said softly and amazingly he knew that if he chose to unleash his power to its fullest he could do just that, but somehow he knew that he would be skirting vary close to the dark side of the power if did indeed do what he threatened. "But it would cost me much, not just physically but in my soul."

Cate nodded and turned back to her plate, after a few more bites she spoke again, "Maybe that is why you had to rest for so long. To bring a sense of perspective to what you could do."

"Just because I can do something," James added. "Does that mean I should?"

He let his gaze land on both women for a moment, holding their eyes against their ability to turn away and then released them with a nod. Cate and Keena both gasped as they tore their eyes from him and looked down at the plates before them, all thoughts of hunger suddenly gone in the realization that he could snuff them out with a thought.

The rest of the evening passed quietly and James went to bed early.

Cate sat for a long time at the table turning the nights events over in her mind. She let her fingers slide across the bow constructed by the strange power of magic and it seemed that she could feel the inner power contained in the weapon. Despite the fear that filled her when James had held her will in the palm of his hand she knew deep in her heart that he would not have allowed himself to hurt her. What she wondered now was if she could do the same, could she hold a person's life in her hands and simply turn away from using the power against them? She thought she could but given the opportunity would she? It was this thought that haunted her dreams that night as she slept fitfully a dozen steps from where James slept peacefully.

* * * * *

The next morning came and found Keena at the edge of the camp watching the cattle stir from the night's sleep. Her experience of the night before had shaken her but not to the point where she would turn her back on her quest. The good of her people came first, and it was that belief that told her that given the chance, she would do what was right. Still, the weight of the power that James must feel was overwhelming and she pondered if her mind would stand the strain. Could she temper her responses with care for those who did her wrong as James had done in Kentuck? Or would she destroy those who wronged her people with not twinge of guilt? It was this that left her pondering the sunrise and searching her soul for the answers that she was not sure she could find.

"Keena?"

The dark skinned archer turned to where Cate approached and offered her a smile, "Cate, you look horrible."

Cate smiled and replied, "I feel nasty, and I didn't sleep well."

"Same here, I kept tossing and turning so I came out to watch the sunrise."

Cate looked out across the plains as she seated herself next to the other woman, "And did you search your soul as much as I did last night?" She brushed a stray lock of blond hair from her face and waited for Keena to answer.

"Most likely," Keena said.

"Did you like what you found?"

"I am not sure," Keena admitted. "For me it is the anger against those who wrong my people. I kept asking myself if I came across a situation like the village of Kentuck would I raze them to the ground like they deserve or am I wise enough to give them a second chance."

"Could you?" Cate pressed.

"I don't know," Keena admitted.

"For me it was wondering if I could dominate someone like James did to us last night and then simply turn away." She was silent for a few minutes and then continued. "Just because I can do something, should I?" They sat in silence for another couple of minutes and then rose and made their way back to the remains of last night's cooking fires. Already there was a bustle of activity around the fires and the smell of sizzling strips of beef filled the air.

James met them at the fire and they took their meal in silence, each of the three lost in the continued thoughts from the night before. It was an hour past sun up when John approached them and waved a greeting.

"We are ready when you are," John said. He lowered himself onto a thick log next to them and accepted a plate of food from a nearby cook.

"I am ready," James said. He handed his plate back to the same cook and motioned to his pack on the ground next to his feet. "Can you ladies be ready soon?"

Cate nodded, "I packed last night before I went to bed."

Keena nodded her agreement as she wolfed down strips of meet and took a long sip of water drawn from a nearby barrel.

"How many will ride with us?" James queried.

"Forty riders including myself, so forty three in total," John said. He waited for them to finish eating and then led them across the camp to where a group of grim faced riders waited for them.

"Each of these men lost a child to the shadow men, and each has sworn to follow your orders to the word," John explained. There were three saddle horses without riders and John motioned for them to choose their mounts.

James looked at the horses and decided on the bay mare with long legs and an intelligent look in her eyes. He fastened his pack behind her saddle and swung up into the saddle.

Cate glanced at Keena and saw that the other woman was eyeing the paint gelding so she walked to where a brown mare with curly looking hair waited. The horse eyed her warily for a moment and then huffed at her and looked away. She clambered into the saddle and settled awkwardly atop the beast and looked around uncomfortably.

"Ready?"

"Ready," James called. A glance behind him assured him that both Cate and Keena were mounted and ready if somewhat uncomfortably. John nodded and vaulted atop his horse; he lifted his long lance and whooped loudly. Immediately all eyes turned to him and silence fell across the field.

"To the City on the Lake and the return of our children."

"Our children?" James asked.

John turned and looked at him, "My wife died two years ago and my daughter was taken five days before you arrived."

"We will find them," James said darkly. In his mind anyone who kidnapped children deserved what they had coming to them.

21 Fire in the Hole

It took them five days of steady riding to reach the outskirts of what had been Chicago and James found his mood growing dark the closer they rode to the ruined city. The sky grew dark and high above them the sun faded until a thick layer of clouds covered the sky. They rode up the remains of interstate 65 and were about ten miles from Lake Michigan when the ruins suddenly rose from the ground and surrounded them with the shattered remains of homes and businesses.

"It's a ghost land," Cate whispered. Despite the low tone of her voice the sound carried along with the muted thud of hooves. She shivered despite the warmth in the air and huddled lower in the saddle as she pushed her mount closer to James.

James was shocked when they finally reached the shores of the great lake and he was able to see the full extent of the destruction. To the west along the shores of what remained of Lake Michigan the skeletal structures grew in size and scope until far out in the distance the smoking remains of skyscrapers still touched the skies. Across the lake surface steam rose and near the remains of downtown Chicago, the lake boiled fiercely.

"What happened to the water?" James asked.

"I don't know," John replied. "It has boiled in that spot every time I have seen the lake."

They camped that night and James soon realized why people avoided the area. The sounds echoing from the surrounding city kept them all sleeping lightly and the occasional scream that echoed across the water sent shivers down his spine. It was an hour before sunrise when James decided that he could no longer sleep, so he rose and walked down to the water. After nodding to the alert rider keeping watch near the water's edge he walked to the east as he let his senses drink in the sights in the distance. Near the western edge of Lake Michigan the rumblings of an underwater volcano added an eerie orange glow to the water and thick steam vents of sulfur fouled the water so badly that no life survived in its murky depths.

With a shudder James let his senses retreat from the water and suddenly he noticed the feeling that he was being watched. It took him several moments to locate the source of the feeling but when he did he was surprised to see the figure of a young man hiding behind the remains of a nearby McDonalds. The sign with the golden emblem still stood proudly looking down at the destruction around it. Two great golden arches of plastic that survived the equivalent of world war three.

"Can I help you?" James asked. He turned slowly and took several steps closer to the figure. Quickly two more figures joined the first together they flattened against the ground unsure if he was talking to them.

"We mean no harm," James tried again. Finally one of the men stood and took a slow step towards him, his eyes darted around as though assuming James was ready to attack him.

"Why have the range men come?"

James glanced across the three hundred yards of beach to where the men of his force were beginning to stir from their sleep. "We come seeking what was taken from them."

"You are talking about the children."

"Yes," James answered in surprise. "How did you know?"

"You are not the only ones seeking the return of your small ones."

"How many were taken from your people?"

"Ten," the man answered.

"What is your name?"

"Saul," he answered. "But the children are not here anymore. They have been moved."

"Well, Saul, you and your two friends," James paused as he widened his senses and recounted. "I mean twelve friends should come with me. There might be a way for us to help each other."

Ten minutes later James and John squatted on their heels across from Saul and listened to his story. Saul was a short man as was each of the men with him. All had black hair and the hue of their skin spoke of a mixed Asian ancestry. From the dark hair to the slight curve of their eyes they reminded James of a friend of his from Hong Kong.

"We searched the city," Saul said. Carefully he adjusted the staff he carried and drew his cloak close around his shoulders to ward off the sudden chill wind that sprang up from the east. "After days of searching, finally we took several captives and questioned them; they told us that the shadow men and their monstrous allies moved the children west yesterday morning."

"Get the mounts ready," John ordered. "We can still catch them if we hurry."

"What else can you tell us?" James asked as a bubble of activity erupted around him.

"The man we questioned said that something happened a few days ago that sent the shadow men into a frenzy," They immediately severed all their connections with the local groups and readied their captives to travel.

"About the same time they lost one of their fellows," James said grimly. "Seems that they know what happens to others that are like them. Can you ride?" It seemed that whoever was controlling the shadow men had a connection that he did not understand.

"Poorly," Saul admitted. "We have few horses and we use those that we have to help grow food."

"Well, we will mount your men behind ours and then we will run those rats down," James declared. He motioned Cate over, "Pack up our things, we need to move fast. The shadow men are moving."

"We will be ready before they are done saddling the mounts," Cate replied. With a worried look on her face she turned and jogged to Keena who was rolling up their blankets. Together they packed the leather bags and ran to where the range men held the reins of their mounts and tied off the bags.

"Saul, you come with me," James ordered. "Is that staff the only weapon you have?"

"Oh, this is not just a staff," Saul replied. He smiled and displayed a wide leather belt strapped around his waist under his cloak. With a deft flick of his fingers he slipped the belt open and it revealed a double row of long darts. "It is a blow gun first and staff second. Each of the darts is coated in a paralyzing poison that works against most creatures very fast."

"Impressive," James said. With a thankful nod to the rider that brought his mare over he swung into the saddle and then reached down to help Saul swing unto the horse behind him. "Where were they headed?"

"According the man we questioned the creatures have a newly constructed hive northwest of the city. He believed that they were headed towards that hive."

"How do you know that he was telling the truth?"

Saul barked a short laugh, "Because he gave his life answering my questions. If your children are involved then you surly understand how desperate my people are."

James shuddered slightly even as he nodded and motioned John to lead them west and north around the city, "Skirt the city and avoid everything." He did not want to chance a battle with the locals and lose men if it could be avoided.

The leader of the range men nodded and motioned his men to follow him. They rode all day at a canter stopping often to swap the extra riders from mount to mount. At that pace it still took them two days of hard riding to reach the north side of Chicago and pick up the trail of the fleeing shadow men and their ant creatures.

"Big group?" commented John as he looked at the churned earth.

"This is the old interstate ninety," muttered James.

Cate looked at him questioningly but when he waved her off. She shrugged and turned back to where John had dismounted and was letting his horse drink from a small pond formed in the remains of a meteor crater impact site. She was starting to get used to his odd comments about what had been.

Saul dismounted and walked to where the tracks were now leading them almost directly west. "I would say about sixty children, and a dozen or so of the ant creatures."

"Can you track a shadow man?" James asked suddenly.

"They don't leave any marks that I know of," Saul said. "The only way to see them is to light the area well and watch for distortions like when the sun warms something on a hot day."

They continued west for half of that day until the group suddenly swung north and cut across the remains of what in years past had been vast tracks of fertile fields. As they rode James remembered driving the interstate through this area and watching field after field of corn slip by his driver's window. He vividly remembered the sounds of his son watching a movie in the back seat while his wife chatted on her cell phone.

"They camped here," Saul said suddenly. He squatted on his heels and pushed his fingers into an indention in the soil. "Small tracks here, wearing hard boots."

James blinked twice realizing that he had no idea what the shorter man had just said. "What was that?"

"They camped here." Saul repeated. "I would say last night."

"That means we are closing the gap," James said thoughtfully.

Saul nodded and fell silent as they continued along the track.

"Where do your people live, Saul?" James asked suddenly over the thunder of the hooves.

"East of the lake away from the smell of the sulfur and dead fish. There are many trees there and we make our homes in the deepest parts of the forest," Saul explained. "That may have been our undoing; there are many shadows in the deepest parts of the forest."

"Hmm, so, central Michigan really," James muttered, then he continued louder. "Doesn't it get cold there in the winter?"

"Not too bad. My father told me stories that his father told him. The winters in this area used to be much worse but since the heavens burned the weather changed," Saul explained.

They rode for almost another day north when John raised his hand and called a halt, "There in the distance just north of us."

James looked to where he pointed and noticed the small cloud of dust almost immediately. "We have half a day to catch them. Let's keep moving." John nodded and motioned his men forward again. This time the hardy mounts moved at a fast canter eating away the distance that still separated the trackers from their prey.

"When we reach them let Saul and his men to the ground," James ordered during a brief break in pace. "They can fight better from there and the same for myself, Cate and Keena. We will form a defensive area for the riders to drive the creatures towards.

The men around him nodded and then took up the chase again. When they finally mounted the last shallow hill separating them from the fleeing party, the sun was beginning to descend towards the horizon and already the harvest moon hung high in the sky.

"There they are, get us close and then drop us off!" James shouted. With a cry the men around him pushed their weary mounts forward at a gallop circling right and left around the fifteen or so skittering Gyants. Near the center of the formation James saw a huddled mass of small figures that looked up at the sudden eruption of war cries and the screamed warnings of their monstrous captors. What was even worse, was on the horizon about two miles further up the highway bed to the north he saw the ominous silhouettes of two pillars marking the creature's base of operations.

"Don't let them break free!" James shouted as two of the Gyants broke from the group and raced north. Immediately ten riders gave chase and rode the two down pinning them to the ground with a dozen strikes of their lances.

Suddenly his attention was back to the ground before him as he completed circling the fleeing group and jumped off his horse. He dropped the reins hoping the mare would survive and motioned Cate and Keena to join him. They happened to stop atop a tiny hill in the middle of the flat remains of a field and James gathered his power around him as best he could. The first assault was a group of four Gyants and the first collapsed to the ground as Saul and his men fired their blowguns with pinpoint accuracy finding niches in their armor where James believed none to exist. The second sprouted two arrows in its head as Cate and Keena loosed their own shafts against the creatures. The next two creatures leapt over the bodies of their comrades and Saul's small force scattered, only one of the men was too slow and his body disappeared under a flurry of slashing pincers.

"No!" James cried. He loosed a stream of fire against the two creatures and let the flames wash across them until they stopped moving. The moment the fire faded he stumbled back weakly, the horded energy of the last few days leaching away from him.

"Are you alright?" Cate cried as she put a third shaft into one of the Gyants that was still struggling weakly to get to its feet. The sickening smell of burnt flesh filled the air and left her fighting off a gag as her stomach threatened to empty itself.

"Yes, but doing something so against nature takes alot out of you," James explained. Using his staff as a prop he hoisted his body back to his feet and then turned to where Saul's men were drifting back into a forward position. In the distance, four or five of the creatures guarding the children were downed and so were several of the range men.

"Look out!" Saul screamed suddenly. One of his men cried out as a shadow moved before him and then faded into the movements of a passing cloud. The short warrior collapsed to the ground trying weakly to staunch the flow of red the dripped from four separate wounds.

"We need light," James growled. Gathering his strength he sent globes of light zipping across the prairie until the area glowed with the light of the sun despite the clouds blocking the real sun. Everywhere he saw a shadow he sent a ball of light and banished the darkness.

'There!" Cate cried as she loosed an arrow.

James whirled to watch her shaft as it flew across the knee high grass, he spotted the shadow man quickly and directed Saul's blow guns against the creature until it slipped to the ground covered in its own blood. They killed two more of the shadow men in quick succession and then the grassy field fell silent.

James leaned heavily on his staff as he kept the area lit with the brilliance of the midday sun. Only when they were certain that the last of the shadow men were dead did he let the light fade back to normal. "I think they are dead," James muttered weakly. He looked from Cate to Keena and motioned back to the south. "Let's go meet up with the others." In the distance the range men finished the last of the

Gyants and were helping the children unto the backs of their horses.

The reunion between the lost children and the parents was joyous but short, with the looming shadows of the earthen pillars John chaffed against the delay until they were ready to move again.

"Are you coming with us?" John asked as James stood next to his mare watching them turn south.

"No, my path lies north and west," James replied. "And I mean to remove at least this colony if I can before leaving this area."

"Will we see you again?" John asked. Behind him the last of the riders trotted off leaving him and his son standing next to their horse watching James and the two women prepare their own horses.

"I will try but I do not know what waits for us in Minnesota," James admitted. "But I would like to return. I still want to see that book of knowledge that your father holds so dear."

"Oh about that," John turned to his rough leather saddles bags and rifled through the interior until he found what he wanted. Reverently he removed a thick leather volume from the bag and offered it to James. "Dad had a copy made for you. He said to give it to you if you after I freed my son."

"Thank you very much," James said. He accepted the gift solemnly knowing what the plainsmen had gone through in the last few weeks and what more they would be exposed to if the Gyants continued to press east. "Good luck to you and ride safely."

They parted with a firm handshake and a quick embrace from Cate and Keena, John's son clung to his father even after they had mounted their stallion and moved south after the rest of the mobile force. James watched them for a while until he finally turned and swung his leg over his saddle. He stored the book of knowledge safely in his saddlebag next to the codex and then pointed his horses north towards the three spires.

"What are you going to do?" Cate asked. She pushed her horse up beside his and turned her piercing eyes to look at him.

"They don't respond well to fire we know. I wonder what it would take to wash the tunnels under the spires with fire."

"From how you responded after burning those other two it would take more then you have," Cate said honestly. She had watched his near collapse after just a few minutes of summoning the liquid fire and she doubted he could sustain the amount of fire it would take to clean the tunnels under the spires.

"Well, the interstate is just east of us. Let's swing over there and check for more of those big rigs." James suddenly had an idea that he thought might work but it would require a bit of luck. They rode for nearly an hour before they located the remains of a semi truck that survived fairly intact.

"Hold on, let me check the tanks," James said. He slipped from his saddle and walked to where the chrome bulldog still marked the nose of the Mack truck. When he tapped the big gas tank he was rewarded with a solid thump that told him the metal was still intact. It took him a bit of power to remove cap and ascertain that the tank was still full and the smell told him that the gas had survived in some form or another.

"Give me a piece of cloth."

Cate tossed him a rag from her pack and watched as he carefully dipped it into the tank until it reached the remaining diesel. When it was soaked completely he tossed it on a spot of dirt and motioned them to stay back. She nearly jumped out of the saddle when James dropped a tiny bit of fire on to the cloth and it erupted in flame.

"Well it is still flammable." James smiled as he used his power to remove the tank from the truck and lighten it enough so that they could move it easily. As they rode north back to where the spires pierced the sky James worked his magic on the tank and its contents slowly. He adjusted properties of the tank so that it was hard but brittle and then in what was even a more tricky process he changed the properties of the gas until it more resembled gel then liquid. He knew the idea behind napalm but he had never seen it used and hoped what the tank now contained was close to the real stuff.

"What do you have planned?" Cate asked finally. The spires were about five hundred yards away now and still no activity was seen around them.

"I am going to float the tank right over the big spire in the middle and drop it." James gave a little more of his power and moments later he held a rough torch that he knew would hold a flame even as it fell. "But I am going to need someone to climb up there and drop this torch while I try and keep the tank moving in the right direction." Already the efforts of the day were making him sluggish and he doubted he could do both without falling asleep.

"I will go," Keena volunteered.

"No, I will," Cate countered almost immediately.

"No, you will stay here with that bow of yours and keep any Gyants away from me and James." Keena raised her hand to ward off Cate's protests. "You're a much better shot then I am and you know it." Despite the bravado in her voice her hands shook as she smoothed the edge of her shirt and eyed the nearby clay mounds.

Cate fell silent and finally nodded. "Alright, just make sure you come back alive. I don't think I can keep him out of trouble by myself." Keena smiled at her and hugged her briefly; they had developed a relationship that most sisters would be proud of over the last few days.

James shook his head as they talked as though he was not even present, "I am sitting right here, you know." He shook his head when they smiled at each other but ignored him. "Alright, get ready. I am going to try to make this quick."

Keena took the torch from him and the lighter, and with a worried look at them she turned and ran smoothly towards the middle spire. As she ran she let her eyes flicker over the surrounding area. Each of the lesser spires was little more than a column like pillar of mud nearly thirty feet tall. The center spire was closer to fifty feet tall and it was as big around as the ruined building they had seen in the City on the Lake. Thankfully the sides were ramped and she was able to run half way up the spire before she was forced to scramble for footholds. The surface of the spire was rough and she had little trouble finding handholds until finally she was perched precariously over a yawning black hole leading down into the ground.

"Keena watch out!" Cate suddenly shouted. She drew her bow back and sent a shaft racing against the Gyants that appeared suddenly from the far side of the spire. Her first shot went wide and broke into a thousand pieces against the hardened clay. The second arrow struck the creature full in its back and drew its attention away from where Keena looked about worriedly for something with which to defend herself.

"Almost got it," James grunted. Sweat streamed down his face as he centered the tank over the entrance and then finally released his hold on it. He opened his eyes to see the enraged face of a giant Gyants racing at him. Suddenly one of the massive eyes sprouted a shaft and the creature stumbled to halt. As the Gyants tried to yank the arrow from its eye several things happened at once. First the tank struck something and James shouted for Keena to drop the torch but oddly he thought the tunnel was much shallower then he imagined it would be.

He thought about shouting for Keena to stop but when he saw the flare of fire and her arm dropping the flame he knew it was too late.

"Keena run!" James shouted. Desperately he wished he could move her away from the coming explosion. Suddenly there was a flash of light and a thunderclap that left his ears ringing. James looked around wildly and noticed that Keena was now sitting on the ground next to her mount with a dazed look on her face. He swayed dangerously in the saddle and then slipped to the ground; drunkenly he stumbled to her and helped her to her feet.

"What happened?" Keena said groggily.

"I don't know but we need to get you into the saddle."

Keena grabbed the pommel of her saddle and dragged herself up until she managed to grip her reins while James stumbled back to his own mount.

"Let's go, I think this is about to get really ugly." He reined his mare around and kicked her hard with his heels. They galloped away to the south not stopping until a sudden thumping sound filled the plains. James turned his head and watched with amazement as all three spires erupted from the ground and liquid fire rolled out of the remains. Dozens of the Gyants covered in fire were hurled hundreds of feet into the air and little remained when they struck the ground.

"Look at that," James said suddenly. His vision swam as he struggled to clear his head but it finally cleared. "I think they are more like ants then we realized at first." From the central spire a gigantic creature pulled itself weakly from the smoking ruins. Fire clung to the queen as she managed to free herself from the general destruction only to collapse on the plains and shudder weakly.

"Man that is one ugly creature," Cate muttered.

James nodded his agreement and instantly his head pounded with pain. The queen had a dozen powerful legs that seemed small when matched against her swollen torso. Two long antennas shifted weakly and then went limp against her bulbous head.

"Let's keep moving," Keena finally muttered. "That is one sight I can do without, besides you need to tell me how I covered all that distance to my horse."

James nodded, "I think I transported you somehow." They circled the massive destruction around the spires and headed north along the remains of old interstate ninety. "All I remember is wishing there was some way I could help you escape and suddenly here you were." James suddenly yawned immensely and swayed dangerously in the saddle. "I think..." he muttered. "I am going to fall asleep." And with those words he felt himself falling from the saddle and darkness closed in around him. He thought he heard a shout but his mind refused to wake up and finally stopped fighting it and embraced the dreams.

22 Wilds of Wisconsin

"Catch him!" Cate cried suddenly. She urged her mount over to where James was muttering under his breath and swaying wildly in his saddle. With Keena's help they lowered him to the ground and tried unsuccessfully to wake him.

"I think he is just sleeping," Keena said finally. She leaned forward and listened closely at James's mouth. "He is breathing."

"The battle and then moving the tank must have left him really weak, ripping you away from danger must have pushed him over the edge," Cate muttered. "I wonder how long he will be asleep."

"Well, I certainly hope it's not for years," Keena grumbled. She stood and looked down at the sleeping form helplessly. "What do we do with him?"

"I guess we could tie him to his saddle," Cate mused. They tried just that but found that James's dead weight was more than they could figure out how to heave back into his saddle so they abandoned that idea.

"What about something that could drag behind the horses?"

Cate nodded, "We just have to find some wood. Then we can use blankets to fashion something."

"Not many trees around here," Keena replied. She turned in a full circle and finally spotted a small stand of trees just north of where they stood. "Over there." She pointed out the stand.

"Let's just toss him over his saddle until we get there," Cate laughed. Working together they maneuvered James over the saddle until he was precariously balanced atop his mare.

"You keep his head and I will watch his feet," Keena said. She stretched out her hand and grabbed James

"Alright," Cate replied. It took them all of the remaining daylight to reach the stand of trees and make a rough camp. The area of trees was larger than they thought and by morning they had constructed a rough sling between two long thick branches. The next morning came with a drizzle of cool rain and it took them an hour to figure out a sling system that would keep the sleeping man from being kicked by the horse. Thankfully the mare was calm and when they finally left the campsite they were able to make good time moving north.

Cate and Keena continued to follow the remains of James had called an interstate for almost four days before James began to stir. Their food supplies ran out on the third day and both of their stomachs were complaining loudly when James finally opened his eyes and looked about. Other then a few stands of berries, the plains were empty except for the occasional prairie dog mound and they scattered when Keena attempted to shoot one.

"How long was I asleep?" he asked as they stooped to unfasten the knots holding him in place.

"Four days," Keena replied as she worked over the makeshift ropes.

"Anything bad happen?"

"No, we stayed on the remains of the road you said would lead us to your home."

* * * * *

It took them nearly two weeks of riding to cross what James remembered as Wisconsin. The sun was high in the sky when they crossed the last bit of ground and entered the remains of Hudson, Wisconsin and looked down at the St Croix River flowing slowly to the south. All around them the peaceful remains of the town were being returned to nature. They saw one small village of fishermen and farmers situated in the remains of the Dells the area of Wisconsin, otherwise, the land that they crossed was empty. James scanned the sky constantly searching for the tell tale plumes of smoke that would mark human settlements but the sky was empty.

The bridge that spanned the river had survived and James urged his mount down the remains of the pavement until he waited at the very edge of the bridge.

"Will it hold us?" Cate asked. She looked about in awe at the massive spanning structure; huge posts driven into the water held the road, as James called it, high above the water.

"I think so," James said as he moved his mare onto the pavement. Some grass and small saplings had taken hold in the cracks opened in the tar but for the most part the bridge seemed sturdy enough. When they arrived safely at the far side James found how close destruction had come to the bridge. About three hundred yards to the west was a thirty-foot crater marking a flat area of the interstate. Many of the craters scattered across the earth had begun to fade and now only appeared as oddly circular depressions in the ground covered in grass and trees.

Five more days of riding brought them around remains of the Twin Cities and sent then north towards Monticello. A few small columns of smoke marked the presence of people in the remains of the once large city but James shook his head when Cate asked if he would stop.

"Not now, there will be time for that later." Highway ten was as crooked as he remembered it, snaking through the northern suburbs of the largest urban area in the northern states. They camped that night in the remains of what had been a Cabala's sporting goods store. James wandered the ground floor but everything of use had long ago been stripped from the shelves and all that remained was rotted bits of cloth and piles of rust. The town of St Michael was a ghost town with just the shattered remains of homes and business slowly rotting away.

James walked out to the tar parking lot and sat down on the remains of a concrete pilling, the rusted remains of a light pole bent off to the side lay on the ground to his left. Half a dozen cars had survived the meteors only to be taken by the relentless progress of time, only one had its windows still intact but the hood was rusted shut. James fiddled with the door handle for a couple minutes as the sun set but when it became obvious that the mechanism was jammed he resorted to his magic to clean the mechanism and break the door loose. A puff of dust erupted from the cracked leather but James was reluctant to use his power on something so frivolous.

Finally he returned to the store and laid down quietly on his blanket, Keena was sitting on her own blanket slowly stirring a pot hanging over the small fire. Cate was returning from a trip to the nearby woods laden down with twigs and logs and she dropped them with a loud thud then slumped to the ground brushing her arms clean.

"Mosquito's are thicker then fleas on a dog out there," she grumbled. A number of red welts rose on her arms already and several more across her face and neck.

"I can help with that I think," James muttered. He carefully placed a small repelling field around their camp and then rolled into his blanket.

"Are you going to eat?" Cate asked. Her tone was worried and she watched his still form with concern.

"Not hungry, just a little tired."

"Want to talk?"

"Not really, no," James replied. "I just need some time to think."

Cate nodded and went back to feeding smaller sticks into the fire; she looked up at Keena who met her eyes with a questioning look. They both shrugged, despite their concern for James they would have to trust that he would be able to solve his inner struggle on his own.

* * * * *

James awoke with a start and looked around him; he was in a richly appointed room with oaken paneling stained with just the slightest bit of rose. He took a deep breath and basked in the smell of fresh wood and just the hint of whatever the builders had used to achieve the rosy wood.

"Nice place," James muttered. He rolled to his side and slipped his feet onto the ground. The mattress under him was firm but it molded to his body like the softest feather bed.

A large armoire dominated one wall, glaring out at any who dared to approach; James chanced the stare and carefully slid the door open. It was empty so he closed the door. He looked down and was happy to find that he was wearing a clean white robe. On the floor near his bed sat a pair of leather slippers so he slipped his feet into them and found that they fit perfectly.

The door opened and closed easily and James stepped into a central room that stretched for at least thirty feet and boasted an arched ceiling held in place by wooden beams of such size that it boggled his mind.

"This is my fortress!" James suddenly burst out. He laughed loudly to himself as he rushed about opening doors and poking into every corner no matter how dark.

"Do you like it?"

James jumped as Rose's voice bubbled up right behind him.

"Rose," James exclaimed. He was so happy with the interior of the fortress that he could only smile and laugh. Much to her surprise James grabbed her and began dancing about the flagstone floor of the main room. They whirled past a massive fireplace set into the northern wall and skirted the edge of a long table polished until it gleamed. Two high backed chairs guarded the ends of the table while four smaller chairs sat subserviently along the sides. James whirled the spirit about until he finally collapsed to the floor.

"I love it!" James exclaimed as Rose sat down on the floor beside him matching his laugh with hers. "It's perfect." Suddenly his smile faded as his mind whirled back to where his physical body lay on earth. "This is almost perfect."

"What's wrong?" Rose asked.

James was unsure if the spirit knew how her mere presence was affecting him, and he squirmed uncomfortably as she leaned close and waited for him to continue. Suddenly he was aware of her smell and the fact that it was from her that the fresh woody smell emanated and the hint of roses surrounded her like a mystery waiting to discover. He rolled to his side and used the movement to gain a bit of distance from her before he turned back and replied.

"On earth I am very close to where I think my family died," he said. "And even though I know there is no way of them surviving as long as I have, I keep hoping that I will walk in and find everything back to normal. I keep hoping and praying that this is a dream."

"But if this is a dream that means that I am not real?" Rose reasoned. "Do you wish that I was not real?"

"No it isn't that at all," James stammered as a hurt look crossed her face. "I love the fact that I have met you but I am still in love with my wife and I have to lay her memory to rest somehow." Dejectedly he drew his knees up and let his head slump down until his face was buried in his knees. "I just want so badly to wake up and find the world back to way it was before..." At first it was a single tear but it soon became a flood as he thought about his wife and son and the terror they must have felt as they watched their world come to an end. The helplessness that they must have felt wondering about what was happening to him and if they would ever see him alive again enveloped him.

As the tremors shook his shoulders he felt a warm arm slip around his shoulder and hold him gently a soft hand stroked his head as a quiet voice whispered words to him that he forgot as soon as they were said. He sat for many minutes basking in the gentle embrace of the spirit woman until without warning the world around him faded from view and a voice called him persistently.

* * * * *

"James!" Cate hissed again. Again the clacking sounds of the Gyants echoed through the building as the carapace of another scout scrapped loudly and sent a pile of bricks clattering across the remains of the concrete floor.

"Oh, what?"

"Shhh," Cate whispered. A deep sigh of relief filled her lungs but she let it out slowly just happy that James was finally awake. "The creatures are here." She pointed to where an ominous shadow moved slowly across the floor towards them.

"Gather up our gear and we will try and get away," James hurriedly rolled his blanket and shoved it haphazardly into his pack. It took under a minute for them to gather up the last remains of their camping gear and then James led them through an opening at the back of the store and into a wide field.

"I don't think they followed us," James said as he watched the store carefully. He probed the store with his mind but failed to find anything that resembled the ant like creatures. "Maybe they went underground already."

Cate nodded, "Would you be able to find them if they were?" She tapped her head indicating she meant with his magic.

"I don't know, I guess I have never tried."

James looked around and took stock of where they were, their mounts were ground hitched nearby so James walked to his mare and fastened his pack behind the saddle. They were mounted moments later and riding along the remains of highway one hundred and one towards Elk River. The road sank between a pair of rolling hills and fifteen minutes later they rode up the last hill and looked out over edge of the town. The Mississippi River still flowed generally in the same place as he remembered but he noticed two huge impact craters that now formed a new pair of lakes fed by the mighty river. The power plant which once fed electrical power into the surrounding homes and businesses was completely gone and as they rode closer James could see where the building collapsed in on itself.

"The power plant took a direct hit," James said. "The series of hits we have ridden by already was probably enough to kill everyone in the immediate area."

"Did you live here?" Keena asked. All around them trees and grass reclaimed much of the city.

"No, further north," James explained. He led them through what remained of the downtown area and he was disappointed to find that not one of the businesses that he remembered had survived. Trees and flowers grew in abundance and even the streets were completely reclaimed. With seemingly dozens of smaller meteor strikes pocking the ground with various sized holes it was nearly impossible to tell where the old city once stood.

"Come on," James urged. He rubbed his face absently and then led them to the north keeping the Mississippi River in view to keep his bearings in the new growth forest. The animal life seemed to have recovered well and they scared up half a dozen deer and one wolf that stared ominously at them before it loped off into the dark shadows cast by the tall pines and up and coming forests of hardwoods.

"Well, this might be a problem," muttered James as he reined in on the remains of the concrete pilings that had once supported the four-lane bridge leading north.

"What?" Keena asked. She let her mount pick its way to the water's edge and drink his fill.

"We are going to get wet," James replied as he removed his outer cloak and tied it to the back of his saddle with his pack. "I will ward the water away from our belongings."

"Can't you just float us across?" Cate grumbled as she removed her light coat and packed it away.

"Well I could but what if I need the power for something more important later?" James countered with a smile at her frown.

Cate stuck her tongue out at him and then stripped away her pants and shirt until the only thing she was wearing was her skin tight armor. James blushed slightly as Keena did the same and then he realized that he could not swim with his long robe on. Suddenly he blushed even more as he was forced to slip out of his robe completely and enter the muddy water wearing only his briefs.

"You know, Keena, he really has a nice set of shoulders hidden under that robe," Cate observed.

"Whatever," James muttered. Rather than enter slowly he plunged into the water and dipped his head under. The liquid was cool but tolerable so he returned to his mare and began coaxing her into the water. She came reluctantly and finally he resorted to using his magic to lightly push the horses until all three were swimming hard for the far side.

"Grab on," James called. Taking his own advice he grabbed his mares stirrup and used her to aid his own crossing. Thankfully the current remained sluggish and they reached the far side easily and since the sun was still high in the sky they lay down on a sandy bit of riverbank and rested in the warm sand until they were completely dry.

"Come on, we are about a day and half ride from home. Whatever shape home is in now." James used a small bit of cloth to brush the sand from his skin and shouldered back into his robe. Cate and Keena waited until he turned his back and then slipped back into their unique under armor and then pulled their over clothes back on and returned to where their mounts waited patiently munching on tall grass. As excited as he was to see familiar surroundings James found that his heart was beating wildly and as he swung into the saddle he willed his heart to calm and tried to steady his shaking hands.

"It will be alright, James," Keena said. "This part of our journey is almost over."

"I just don't know what makes me more nervous. Finally reaching home or just staying away from there."

They rode on in silence and camped on the remains of the concrete overpass that had once carried traffic over the twin railroad tracks running from the Twin Cities to the north. The fields and forests around them were silent all night and only broken by the occasional huffing of deer that caught their scent. James thought that he spotted the yellow eyes of a hunting wolf once but they disappeared so quickly that he wondered if his mind was playing tricks on him.

Matthew J Krengel

23 Quarrians

James slept little that night and the moment the sun kissed the horizon he was in the saddle urging Cate and Keena to hurry as they wolfed down a quick and cold breakfast.

"Coming!" grumbled Cate as she rubbed the sleep from her eyes and stalked to where her mount waited. Even the horses seemed in a foul mood that morning and things got worse almost immediately. Overhead a row of thunderclouds rolled in from the west chasing towards them until the sky opened up and poured buckets of water on them. Within two minutes they were completely soaked to the skin and only James seemed not to care. The rain continued for nearly an hour and then the sun returned unleashing its heat across the land and sending waves of humidity into the air.

The town of Big Lake came and went and James noticed once again that the town and surrounding area took a horrible beating. Where flat fertile fields had once dominated the landscape now new growth forests filled impact craters and rugged abrupt drop offs marked the chaos of the day the sky burned.

Even the lake that had given the town its name had ceased to exist as the water had drained off into the surrounding countryside by the violence of the assault. Now a vast swamp filled the area and acres of bull rushes filled with birds and croaking frogs stretched out for miles. With somber faces they rode on, covering mile after mile at a steady trot until finally James spotted a familiar sight. The massive granite walled reformatory sitting ponderously on the edge of St Cloud had survived. Even more interesting were the multiple plumes of smoke rising from inside the walls that marked the presence of survivors. Multiple fields were arranged around the walls, each marked with farmer's cottages.

"Are you stopping?" asked Keena as she pointed to where a sentry walked along the top of the granite walls.

"Not right now," James replied gruffly, ignoring the village surrounding the old prison.

Keena gave a short wave to the sentry who was staring at them. With a shrug she reined her mount away from the smell of the wood smoke and followed the white robed archeologist turned magician as he direct his mount towards his home.

Overall the town around prison survived better then both Elk River and Big Lake. A scattering of craters and their accompanying devastation marked out a few places but over all, the city had survived remarkably well. It appeared to James that fire had been a worse enemy to the city of St Cloud then the meteors.

"This way," James called. He urged his mount towards the river and crossed his fingers hoping that at least one of the bridges survived the devastation. His heart fell as they reached the first bridge once leading across into the campus of St Cloud State University. All that remained was a single concrete pillar in the middle of the river and the water rushed around the submerged stones and jagged chunks of the fallen bridge. Half a dozen men were fishing along the riverbank and they called out a greeting which James ignored as he pulled his mount around to the north.

"Come on, at one time there were five bridges in this town maybe one of them survived."

"James," Cate called. "Why don't we ask?"

"Come on," James growled. "I will make a bridge if I have to."

The next two bridges were also gone but when James rode a bit further along the banks he saw that the Sauk Rapids bridge survived.

They arrived at the intact bridge a few minutes later and were greeted by a scrambling of men and horses.

"Hold where you are!"

"Great, what now," James growled. A dozen rough looking men with hard leather ran towards them brandishing a motley collection of rough swords and crude spears. Immediately Keena and Cate fitted arrows and drew back their bows ready to fight if the threat continued. "Wait!" James called.

"Hold!" A voice thundered from the front rank and suddenly the men skidded to a halt. Another twenty or so men stationed near the bridge looked nervously at them but held their position as though ready to repel attackers from across the river. James took this all in quickly and then refocused his attention on the tall thickly muscled man who edged forward towards them while motioning his men to wait.

"Who are ye and what do ye want on our lands?"

"My name is my own business and I am simply passing through to where my family once lived," James answered. His voice echoed with the authority he willed into it and many one of the men before him nodded and lowered their weapons.

"I am sorry good master but the Quarrians have their riders patrolling the far side and they have threatened to kill any who cross into their lands."

"My name is James and I am going to cross this bridge whether these Quarrians like it or not," James said. "Who are the Quarrians anyway?" James slipped from his saddle and looped his reins over the horn of Cate's saddle.

"I am Edd, a soldier in the service of the Lord Aren of Graystone Castle." Edd said. He motioned again and all but two of his men turned and trotted back to where they were working to assemble a rough gate to block the crossing. "We have lived many years at peace with the men of Quarry but suddenly a few days ago they accused us of stealing their children and we have been fighting skirmishes with them almost every day."

"Children disappearing?" James asked. He had a sinking feeling in his stomach as he stared longingly at the far side of the river. A mile to the north nestled against the banks of the mighty river was his home or at least the remains of it and he wanted to cross so badly.

"Aye, but they won't listen to us. We told them the same thing has happened to us but they called us liars and attacked anyway."

"The shadow men," Cate whispered.

Edd looked at her suddenly and his face was etched with disbelief. "How could ye know of the shadow creatures?"

"We have seen their handiwork in other places, theirs and their servants the Gyants." James motioned for Cate and Keena to put up their bows, which they did with only a slight look of distrust at the men struggling to lever a thick oak log into place. The great river was running much higher than usual and James asked Edd about it, wondering if the meteor strikes had changed the local climate at all.

"My papa told me that the winter used to be much colder but the river has run this high every year for the past twenty years at least."

James nodded.

"Will you allow us to cross?" James asked. He followed Edd to where his men were lashing the first log into place.

"I would advise against it," Edd repeated. "But since you do not fall under Lord Aren's domain I will not stop you."

James sighed loudly, he wanted very badly to go speak to this Lord Aren and offer his help in rescuing the missing children but his pull to return home was even stronger. Slowly he swung back into the saddle and ignored the cries of irritation from his back and legs.

"Let them through!" Edd called. His men drew back and watched as James, Cate, and Keena guided their mounts around the thick log.

Their mounts hooves clopped loudly as they cross the concrete bridge sections. A few vines had taken root and were spreading across the pillars holding the spans in place but for the most part James thought the bridge itself looked in reasonably good shape. When they exited the concrete sections James found that the forests reclaimed much of the St Cloud side of the river. He turned his mount up river and found a game trail that would take them along the riverbank. Excitement filled him knowing that he was now under two miles from his home, they rode at a trot until they suddenly burst free of the trees and James found he was staring at the massive ruins that had formerly been Super Wal-Mart.

"James," Cate said suddenly. "There are horsemen near the walls over there." Cate slipped an arrow from her quiver and notched it so that she was ready to fire at a moment's notice.

Following her directions he spotted the group of horsemen almost immediately, they were dismounted and clustered around a small fire. Suddenly a shout echoed from the group of forty or so riders and they leaped into the saddle, racing to where James sat on his mare basking in irritation at another interruption. The men were roughly dressed with leather pants and shirts and each carried a small round shield and all carried a sturdy spear. Most of them had long hair tied back from their faces and more than a few had red and brown paint etched across their faces.

"Let me handle this," James said ominously. Already his presence began to swell in the eyes of the men racing towards them and many of their eyes went wide as the men tried desperately to pull their mounts up.

"Men of the Quarry," James thundered. He bit back a partial smile as two of the riders actually fell from their mounts and cowered on the ground. "Why are you trying to pick a fight with powers beyond your comprehension?"

"He is a god."

James heard the whispers but this time he ignored it, "I know that the shadow men have attacked your people and stolen your children but the men across the river have had nothing to do with it and neither have I."

"But my lord, how can we get our children back." Someone called and James closed his eyes for a moment then replied.

"What is your name?"

"Conner, my lord."

"Go back to your people and stop fighting with Lord Aren's men. When I have finished with my business we will come to you and see about finding your kidnapped children." James waved his hand at the men making most of them cringe back in fear. "Now Go!"

The men on the ground scrambled back to their mounts and almost as one they turned and raced away down the wide road leading towards the remains of the city. When they finally disappeared from view James let the image of him slip away and turned to look at Cate and Keena.

"Think I over did that?" James asked.

"Not really," Keena laughed. "I am starting to think that none of the people alive on the earth right now can get along without the threat of force hanging over their heads."

"That may be true."

They rode over the remains of highway fifteen and continued down a narrow deer trail running along the track of the old county road one. They passed the gutted remains of the Sartell paper mill and James noticed the dam was completely swept away and the plant itself seemed to have sustained a massive strike. All that he could see of the pale blue buildings was about half of one of the smaller buildings and some of the concrete used to support where the buildings had abutted the river.

James looked at all of this but his mind was half a mile down the road. As they continued down the remains of the road, the trees began closing in once again and soon they were weaving through a thick growth of new forest. Despair entered into James as he searched the forest for his home through the thick undergrowth. Just when he had begun to believe that there was no chance of finding the dwelling he broke free of the forest and stood in a small clearing. At the middle of the clearing was the two-story brick building that he remembered so fondly. The roof was gone but the walls remained and actually seemed to be in good shape. The attached three-car garage still stood and in this case the roof was still intact so James slipped from the saddle and handed his reins to Keena who was closest.

"Wait here."

Cate and Keena nodded but James was not watching anymore. Already in his mind he was walking across a well-manicured lawn and looking at the tulips and day lilies that his wife loved to plant. The front door was slightly ajar and James walked inside calling out for his wife and son. When no one answered he walked through each room in the home seeing them as they had been and not as they were now.

He heard the music of the baby grand piano that his wife loved but when he entered the music room the piano sat empty. "Karen!" James called over and over. "Johnny, where are you!" he called for his son but still got no answer. Now panic began to take hold of him and he rushed through the house again room by room where the walls had faded and the furnishings had fallen into piles of rotten wood.

He entered the kitchen as the last of his vision failed; only an empty room remained. Slowly he fell to his knees reaching out with his hands as even the last bits of music faded from his mind. His spirit fell and his heart felt heavy, all around him the paint fell from the walls in vast sheets. The tile flooring was broken into hundreds of pieces and the granite counter top from the kitchen island broken in two and lay on the ground in front of him. Dejectedly he slumped to the ground and let his face touch the broken tiles. He lay there on the floor for some time as tears covered the floor around him. His will was failing and it seemed pointless for him to continue on. His wife and child were surely dead even if they had survived the meteor blasts.

"James?" Cate called softly. She slipped by the small section of the metal door that survived the onslaught of time and looked about. The first room was big and the ceiling was at least ten feet tall. A few of the planks were missing in the floor but the rest seemed sturdy enough to hold her weight so she entered the area and walked to where a wide opening led to the back of the house. James was laying on the floor near a second door that led to another part of the house and she hurried to his side.

"Karen?"

"No, James, its Cate," she replied softly. She knew the wrenching feeling of having your family and home taken away and wanted so badly to comfort him.

"Johnny?" James murmured again. Slowly lifting his hand to where Cate crouched before him.

"I don't know who Johnny is," Cate whispered. "But I wish I did."

Suddenly James lifted his head and looked at her with recognition in his eyes. "Can I tell you about them?" he asked. Suddenly his mind was clear again as he pictured his son and wife. When she nodded and sat down next to him he rose slowly to his knees and wrapped his arms around them. "Johnny was eight years old when he and Karen came to the airport and said goodbye to me. His brown hair is cut short and he has my blue eyes but Karen's mouth and nose. We used to sit at the kitchen table and play board games, he loved it. He didn't even care what game it was as long as we sat down together. Sometimes I would pop a big bowl of popcorn. Saturdays we sat and watched cartoons on the floor in the basement; used to drive Karen nuts that we sat on the floor instead of using the couch." On and on James went, remembering his son and wife in every detail that he could dredge out of his mind.

Cate listened to him talk until the sun began to fade, she kept her arm around his shoulder offering her silent support and a listening ear. When James finally stopped talking she helped him stand and together they walked out to where Keena sat near a fire and was cooking supper.

James ate quickly that night and then rolled into his blanket and fell asleep immediately, the emotions of the day draining him of all his strength.

"Is he going to make it?" Keena asked when James had gone to sleep.

"I think so," Cate replied. She sat in the glow of the campfire watching him sleep. "He truly loved his family more than anything else and the fact that he was not here when they died is hurting him horribly. But I think tonight helped him set some of his memories to rest."

Keena nodded as she used a nearby bucket of water to rinse the bits of soup left from their supper away and then dried the small pot and slipped it into her pack. Together, she and Cate watched the stars appear in the night sky and as the fire faded the moon shown so brilliantly to it seemed to be day once again.

24 A Final Letter

The next morning came and went and James slept until the sun was high in the sky. Cate was beginning to worry when suddenly he opened his eyes and looked her, "Good morning, Cate."

"Good morning to you, how do you feel today?" she asked.

"Sad, but much better," James admitted as he helped himself to a cold slice of beef and a chunk of cheese. He ate quietly and then rose to his feet and faced the brick facade of his old home. "I will be right back."

"Do you want us to come with you?" Keena asked.

"You can if you want to," James offered. His mood was much improved from yesterday and he seemed almost happy. "We had a small safe in the basement and I want to check it."

"What is a safe?" Cate asked hesitantly.

"A small steel box with a lock on it," James said. He made a motion with his hands showing the approximate size of the safe and then turned and walked towards the front door. They all entered the building and James led them to the shadow filled stairs leading down into the darkness of the basement area. He lit his small globe of light and wiped the spider webs away with a wave of his hand.

The basement area smelled of mold and most of the carpet was completely rotted away. He walked to the northern most corner and knelt where a small pile of wood was stacked and began moving the bits of remaining paneling and construction lumber. Moments later he revealed the safe set in the block wall. The two inch thick steel door was rusted tight but James could tell that the interior remained dry with a probe from his mind. Rather than waste precious time trying to work the door open he reached out with his magic and easily pulled the safe door off its hinges.

"What have we here?" James muttered suddenly. He recognized the paper as a heavy stationary that his wife routinely used to send him letters when he was out on one of his expeditions. Carefully he encased the folded paper with a field of power that held it together and then unfolded it. Once it was laying flat on the ground he concentrated on restoring the paper and the faded lines of ink that covered it.

"Karen wrote this," James exclaimed. As he read, his heart beat faster, pounding in his chest like a wild beast trying to escape captivity. With a trembling hand he pointed to the date atop the page. "And she wrote it well after the Day the Sky Burned. Look it says Twenty-fifteen. She survived!" James jumped to his feet and hugged Cate and then Keena wildly.

"James, she still can't be alive anymore." Keena pointed out timidly but he waved his hands.

"I know that but if she survived then Johnny might have survived too. If they both survived maybe Johnny found a wife and I have grandchildren somewhere." Hurriedly he knelt by the letter and began reading.

2013: The End

Dear James,

I write this knowing that you will never read it but I must in order to give my spirit peace. You were in Central America when the warning sirens sounded and we hurried to the radio to hear the reports. It appears that the hurricane and other natural phenomenon created so much havoc around the world that no one saw the disaster coming. A meteor shower of such immense size and power hit the earth so that it wiped out most of the human life on the planet. I still do not know how Johnny and I survived but we managed. When we emerged from the house we found the Hones next door still alive and old man Jenner from across the street, but they were the only other people we could find close by. As the dust clouds covered the sky and fires burned off much of the area around us we took refuge at the Sauk Rapids city building, which had survived the shower and the fires. Somehow Johnny and I lived and as the weeks passed, the skies began to clear and summer finally came. The longer we stayed at the city building the more people we found alive and our resources began to run low. In order to survive the decision was made to split up and Johnny and I went north with a group heading towards Duluth. About fifty of us are making the journey, we want to find a place to farm that is safe from looters. I wish you were here so badly, Johnny misses you terribly as do I. James, I love you and I will never stop waiting for you. If some miracle happens and you find your way home someday, come look for us. We will survive somehow and somewhere we will be waiting for you.

Yours forever,
Karen

James slumped back against the musty concrete blocks and scanned the letter again and then placed it carefully next to him on a dry spot of floor. A quick search of the basement told him what he already expected, that it was empty of anything useful. After refolding the letter and placing it in an interior pocket that he created especially for it he climbed the rickety steps back to the main floor and exited the rotted husk of the home.

"What now?" Keena asked.

"Well, we see if we can sort out the situation here and then I am going north to find out if my grandchildren are alive." James turned to where the horses were hobbled and began saddling his mount. Thankfully, Cate had already packed their travel supplies and James strapped the leather pack onto the back of his mount and then swung atop the waiting beast.

They left the remains of James's house and picked their way back through the new growth forest until they reached the remains of highway fifteen. They rode towards where James remembered a crossroads mall once stood and James found that nothing survived this close to town. Apparently a series of smaller strikes leveled much of the immediate area and none of the old buildings could be seen anywhere. Hundreds of smaller trees covered the area as nature went on about her business and slowly destroyed the works of man. Thick carpets of grass covered most of the tar roads and when James dismounted and dug down he found that the tar was still there in many places. Much of it was simply buried under a thick layer of dirt and the root systems of the plants had still not destroyed much of it.

A series of thick plumes of smoke rose into the air as they approached the remains of what James remembered once being called Quarry Park.

"Ha, Quarrians," James laughed. When the two women looked at him curiously he waved a hand towards the smoke. "This area used to be called Quarry Park and it was a place where people would come to relax."

"And after people settled here they took the name Quarrians." Keena reasoned.

"What's a quarry?" Cate asked suddenly when she realized that she had not heard the word before.

"It's a place where people used to cut granite and stone from the earth. Now the hole in the ground is filled with water and with technology gone it would be a perfect source of water."

Cate nodded.

They rode into view of the settlement and found an impressive array of log walls and rough-cut pieces of granite fitted tightly together. The entire wall seemed to enclose an area of nearly thirty acres and arranged around the walls were corrals for horses and an assortment of fields and smaller farmer cottages. Inside the wall James could see a few two-story buildings but most seemed to be single story dwellings and businesses. The distant clang of iron on iron spoke of the presence of a blacksmith and a long building outside the wall surrounded by hides told him that someone had relearned how to tan leather.

The front gate was open and three men in hard leather caps and jackets motioned them to a halt. They carried long rough spears and atop the gate three more men with bows kept careful watch over them.

"We met a man named Conner over near the river and we told him we would come to speak to him when we concluded out business. Where is he?" James asked and his tone left no room for argument.

"I am here."

James looked up and saw Conner striding towards them with a number of men in tow behind him. He still had his hair tied back with a leather thong and carried his spear and shield.

"We need to speak."

"Come," Conner motioned. "Your archers... " Conner stammered as if realizing for the first time that both of them were female. "They may accompany you."

James dismounted and handed his reins to one of the guards at the gate and then motioned for Cate and Keena. Conner led them to a long building built of logs and chinked with mud and straw. Inside, a small fire burned in a big central pit adding a bit of warmth and with it some flickering light. In the ceiling a hole let the smoke escape and covering the ground in many places were thick rugs woven of grass and covered with furs.

"Now, then, I will have refreshments brought and we can talk in peace." Conner motioned to one of the men and he bowed his head then turned and disappeared out a nearby door.

"You have a prosperous settlement here," James said when they were all seated on the thick rugs. "But I have heard that there are problems with missing children."

"That is true," Conner said hesitantly. "Over the past month seven children have been taken. Until yesterday we assumed it was raids by Lord Aren of Graystone. Now I don't know, sire, but my people demand action. Despite doubling our watch, every few days another child disappears and there are rumors of fierce looking creatures being spotted south west of the river."

"Have there been rumors of shadows coming to life?" James asked. He believed he already knew the answer but better to be safe and know for certain.

Immediately suspicion leapt into Conner's eyes, "How can you know that!" he demanded. Several of the men standing nearby leveled their spears and Cate and Keena quickly notched arrows expecting the worse.

"Stop!" James thundered. He immediately employed the same tactic as before and his image seemed to swell in front of all those present. The fire burning brightly in the pit behind them suddenly burst to life and flames nearly licked the ceiling suddenly banishing the shadows. James spotted what he thought he had felt the moment the flames erupted and he used his power to grab a spear from a stunned soldier and sent it hurtling across the room and slamming into the shoulder of the spying shadow man.

"Cate, shoot it," James cried.

Her quick eyes spotted the struggling creature almost as fast as James and her arrow was already in flight. By the time James's words died there was a flurry of movement as Conner's men surrounded the shadow man and he faced a ring of weapons. In what moments before had been a dark corner the shadow man struggled weakly to remove the spear and arrow from its body until it finally ceased its struggles and collapsed to the floor.

"Quickly, grab it," James thundered. "We may have a moment to glimpse its base before it dies completely."

Keena dropped her bow and charged to the still struggling figure, she grabbed the shadow man by the leg and pulled it towards the fire, which suddenly returned to its normal size leaving Conner and his men rubbing their eyes.

James knelt swiftly next to the creature and sent his senses probing into the creatures mind. This time, a wall of blackness that blocked his every attempt to penetrate it, met him. He struggled for many long minutes until the shadow man's breathing ceased and all of its memories died with its last breath. As the death throes took the creature James caught a sense of a strange power guarding the creatures and mocking his attempts to penetrate the wall of darkness that sealed its mind away.

"What did you see?" Keena asked. Gracefully she walked back to where her bow and arrow lay on the floor and retrieved them from the ground. In its last struggles the shadow man had slashed at her with razor sharp claws that tore her outer clothes to shreds.

"Are you alright?" James asked. Ignoring the now dead body at his feet he crossed to her and examined the shredded clothing across her upper legs.

Keena shrugged. "Didn't feel a thing, at least we know that this armor you made us can stand up to a shadow man's claws."

"Sadly, I think whoever sent out this creature realized what I did last time and was guarding its mind against just such an attempt," James growled. With a last glance at Keena's shredded trousers he waved his hand at them and mended the seams and brought a round of gasps from Conner and his men.

"So, what do we do?" Cate asked.

"I am not sure," James admitted. "Conner come here and see the face of your nemesis." James motioned to the still body on the flood and then seated himself on a nearby cushion and tried to clear his mind.

"What is it?" Conner asked. He nudged the shadow man with his toe unsure if he was safe or not.

"It's safe," James said. "I do not know how they were made but they are flesh and blood just like us. They are the things that have been taking your children and the reason that doubling your guard did no good. Where they come from, that I do not know."

"How do we stop them?" Conner asked. He quickly overcame his initial fear of the creature and he now knelt beside it and used his fingers to examine the garish wound.

"I took that one by surprise with the burst of fire but we were lucky." James rose and walked to where the ruler of the Quarrians knelt next to the creature. "We managed to kill one far to the south where it and its Gyants were doing the same thing they are doing here. Stealing the children of the survivors."

"Gyants?" Conner asked.

"Just what it sounds like," Cate explained. "Really big ant like creatures, even the smallest gyant is almost the size of your horses and with armored hides and big pincers. The bodies are that of an ant but the torso seems almost human looking but warped beyond belief."

"That is what the outlying farms have seen then," Conner said. He walked back to where the single chair in the room sat and threw himself down into it. "What do we do? How can we fight something we can't see or something as big as you say these Gyants are."

"Torches," James muttered. "Put out a lot of torches with your sentries and if you see the Gyants shoot arrows at the heads or backs if you can get around behind them. Our allies to the south found that heavy spears with broad heads can pierce their hides."

"That still doesn't solve our biggest problem," Keena pointed out. "We have to find the children and this time we don't have a lead like we did last time."

"I think it is time for us to talk to Lord Aren and form some sort of an alliance between the Quarrians and Graystone."

Conner frowned at James like he had mentioned something almost as foul as the shadow man, "Must we talk to the pompous moron?"

"By the time this is done we may need every ally we can find." James pointed out. "Besides, Graystone has the same problem you do and if you don't come together to solve it I may get very irritated." James was not normally a man given to threats but the bull headedness of the survivors was getting on his nerves.

Conner gulped uneasily.

"Also, if you won't form some sort of an alliance I will simply move on about my business and leave you to your problems." James knew in his heart the threat was an idle one but no one else did and that made it effective.

Cate glanced at him momentarily but when she saw the determined set in his face she read it for what it was. He would do all that he could to help these people despite his lingering threats.

"Fine, we will meet him."

James nodded, "How soon can we arrange the meeting?"

"Two days," Conner replied. "It will take me that long to try and get a message through. Our two peoples are not on the best of terms right now." After a few second of silence he added sheepishly. "I may have had something to do with that."

James simply nodded and then added, "That will work out well enough. I wish to ride through the surrounding area and see if I can pick up any problems. I trust that we will be given free rein to ride where we like."

"Of course," Conner replied.

25 Atwood Center

The next two days James spent riding through the remains of down town St Cloud and witnessing the combined power of heavenly wrath and nature put to work against the creations of man. Most of the buildings had taken a series of hits and little remained but a layer of broken glass, crushed bricks, and chunks of concrete with rusted rebar sticking out at weird angles. Much of the remains were layered under a thick coating of vines and stunted trees trying to send their roots deep into the ground and failing. He rode as far as the remains of the university and was surprised to find several buildings had survived intact but lacked the time to explore then fully. He decided to return later.

"What a bleak sight," Cate commented as they looked on the remains of the library and framed behind it the low concrete building called Atwood center.

"It probably survived as well as it did because of the concrete and steel." James rode as close as the broken out glass doors and leaned over his saddle to peer into the darkness. He sent his light dancing down the hall for twenty feet but only succeeded in scattering a host of nocturnal creatures. Half way down the passage his light winked out suddenly and James stared down into the darkness curiously. He had never seen his magic fail before but it hardly worried him, when he concentrated again the globe popped back to life next to him.

They left the campus and rode east, passing by the single wall that was all that remained of the old Speedy building along with a few dozen rusted lumps that had once been delivery trucks. The rest of the building was a jumbled pile of rust pitted girders and the accompanying vines that seemed to flourish in the ruins. James turned back when he reached the still intact overpass where interstate ninety-four once carried thousands of automobiles each day.

Here and there they saw the rough log homes and stone chimneys of farmers tending fields where the land remained flat. Plowing was done as it had been for a millennium before the invention of tractors by heavily muscled work horses pulling the iron plows accompanied by the farmers. Most of the people they saw were friendly and seemed always ready to offer a smile or a drink of cool water. However, under the surface James sensed an under-current of nervousness as evening began to fall. As the sun set fully he saw a farmer hustle his small daughter into the house and watched as the man closed the heavy shutters and listened as he slid blocking bars in place around each of the small cottages entrances. It was then that James felt the chill of the night close in around him and for some reason a feeling of dread came across his heart. He glanced at Keena and Cate and saw that they both shuddered at almost the same time.

"Something evil is afoot tonight," Keena muttered.

"I felt it too," Cate admitted. 'We should return to Quarry."

It was fully dark when they arrived back at Quarry, four men and eight torches watched the gates but they were allowed passage immediately. Conner met them at the log hall with a worried look on his face.

"What happened?" James asked.

"My nephew and six others disappeared before the gates closed tonight. None of them have been heard from or seen for some time now," Conner explained. "I sent men to search every corner of the town but no one has found any of the missing children. Please, James we must act now."

"We will ride to Graystone tonight and try to meet with Lord Aren. Gather together as many men as you can without weakening your defenses here and meet me at the bridge close to where we first met."

Conner nodded, "We will move all the people into the hall and concentrate the guard here. Then we can field almost three hundred men."

James swung back into his saddle and motioned for Cate and Keena to follow him, "Come, I think we must take care of this tonight or we may not get a chance again."

"Lead on" Keena said. Already she was in her saddle with her bow out and ready to fight.

The moon was full in the night sky as they galloped back down the grassy remains of the Division Street towards the river. Rather than loop towards the still standing bridge James led them straight towards the old prison now called Graystone.

"James, the bridge is out," Cate called over the thunder of their horse's hooves.

"We will not need it," James cried. His blood was racing and he could feel power flowing through him. They arrived at the river and James did not slow his mount or allow the women's mounts to slow. His horse snorted wildly but raced on across a bridge of thin air that suddenly became as hard as steel. Cate screamed behind him and he heard Keena cursing loudly until they touched down on the far side.

"You could have warned us!" Keena cried as they raced towards Graystone.

James smiled but kept his eyes focused on the road before them, until they reached what had once been Minnesota Boulevard. The granite walls that encircled the old prison now encompassed the entirety of what had been the parking lots and the wedge of land was nearly twenty acres in size. A wide gravel track broken now and then by sections of tar led up to an imposing gate lit by a dozen torches. The walls connected to the gatehouse were nearly thirty feet tall and built of granite but broken here and there by sections of timber and it was obvious that the walls were an ongoing construction project.

"Halt!"

A voice rang out loudly in the night air and James pulled his mount to a halt in the sickly light cast by the smoky torches. Half a dozen nervous faces stared down at them and the same number of arrows pointed in their direction.

"I must speak with Lord Aren immediately!" James called. Under him the mare he was riding panted heavily as she labored to regain her breath.

"No one passes through the gates after dark." The barely visible watch man called.

"Look you fool," James thundered. "Unless I miss my guess you have experienced a rash of missing children this evening just as night fell. If you do not act now you will never recover any of them."

A gasp echoed out over the gates and moments later a smaller postern gate slipped open and Edd walked out.

"Edd, we must act now. The Quarrians are gathering their soldiers even now. They suffered seven more missing tonight and I am willing to bet that you have lost at least that many."

"Twelve," Edd said slowly. "And my own daughter is among the missing."

"If we are to find them we must act now," James urged. "I must speak with Lord Aren."

"I will take you to him," Edd said. "Open the gates!"

The moment they cleared the gates the men on watch hurried to close the massive portals again and close what the creatures they all knew were waiting to rush through.

"You need to light more torches and gather everyone into a central area where all the entrances and exits can be barred," James commented. Edd led them at a run through the wide street leading from the gate to the granite building that long ago marked the entrance to the prison. Twenty men in burnished chain mail kept watched scattered around the building half armed with rough but sturdy crossbows and the rest carrying swords and shields. Immediately all eyes turned to watch them as Edd rushed forward and spoke to a tall severe looking man with dark eyes and a thin beard.

"Captain Lews will take us to see Lord Aren," Edd said when he returned breathlessly to them. "But he wishes you to assure him that you are not in league with the shadow men."

"Captain," James nodded. "If I were in league with the Shadows you would not be alive right now."

"I have twenty soldiers here, you could do nothing to stop us if we decided to kill you," Captain Lews scoffed. "I am not as easily cowed as armsman Edd."

James called forth a dozen globes of light and bathed the front of the castle in light that rivaled the power of the sun, "Captain, we are wasting time."

Captain Lews blinked suddenly as many of his dropped their weapons to the ground and tried to block the light from their eyes. Ignoring the sudden burst of outcries James scanned the area searching for the faint outline that would betray the presence of a shadow man to him.

"I do not see any, James," Cate called from the left and Keena quickly echoed the words on the right.

"Who are you!" a deep voice thundered suddenly.

James allowed all but two of the lights to wink out and refocused his eyes to the glass doors that somehow survived for nearly a century at the front of the building. A tall athletic man stood just outside the portal glaring at them and holding a long deadly sword in a tight grip so that his knuckles shown white. He wore a shining shirt of mail and his long hair was tied back from his face revealing high cheekbones and hawkish eyes that glared at them angrily.

"Lord Aren." James swung down from his saddle and offered a shallow bow. "My name is Dr James Kaning and I know of the shadow men. Indeed, I have seen their foul hands at work in other places. I also know that just tonight you and the Quarrians have lost almost nineteen children to these foul creatures. Without my help you stand no chance of regaining them."

"The Quarrians are liars and not to be trusted. How can I know that they did not take the children themselves and send you as an assassin to kill those of us who will not bow to whatever they wish?"

"You fool," James said suddenly. His voice dropped and a dangerous note entered it that made the men now clustered around Lord Aren take an involuntary step backwards. "You would sacrifice the lives of all those taken just to remain a closed minded idiot. Show yourself a real leader of these people and look out for the good of your people."

Lord Aren's face turned deadly white and he took a deep breath, for a moment James thought he was going to order his men to attack. After what seemed like an eternity Aren let the breath go slowly between clenched teeth and the color returned to his skin.

"What do you want me to do?"

"I have spoken to the Quarrians and they are gathering their people into a central location to defend them more easily. Conner is sending three hundred horsemen to the bridge where I met your men. How many men can you gather quickly without leaving your people at risk?"

Lord Aren thought silently for a moment. "Tomorrow I could offer you five hundred but on short notice two hundred. We have few mounts here though, they will be on foot."

"As long as they can fight," James muttered. "I have a feeling that we will need all the help we can get before tonight is done."

Lord Aren motioned to Captain Lews, "Go gather everyone in the castle and barricade the doors. Then get everyone who can fight armed and gathered at the gates."

"Yes sir," Captain Lews turned and rushed off into the night. Less than a minute later a warning bell began to toll in the darkness.

"Lord Aren, have your people noticed anything strange going on around the countryside?" James asked. Despite gaining the cooperation of both rulers he still lacked a location to direct his rescue mission.

"Nothing that I can recall." Lord Aren replied. Carefully he slid his still naked blade back into its scabbard and walked to where James searched his mind for some way to find the missing children.

"My Lord?"

A voice broke in hesitantly and James glanced up to see Edd edging closer with a hopeful look on his face.

"What is it?" Lord Aren asked somewhat impatiently.

"When we were dispatched two days ago to construct the barrier some of us heard strange sounds coming from across the river."

"Most likely Quarrian spies keeping watch for our army," Lord Aren said dismissively.

"No wait," James broke in. "From where exactly?"

"That low gray building across the river," Edd explained. "It is half covered with vines now but it is the only building that survived the day the sky burned in that area."

"The old Atwood building," James muttered.

"Is that the one where your light died mysteriously?" Cate asked suddenly, breaking her long silence.

"It was," James agreed. "We need to get back there as fast as we can. With as many torches as your men can carry."

"I know that area," Lord Aren said. "I can have my men there quickly."

"We will ride ahead and gather Conner and his men," James explained as a plan began to form in his mind. "When we arrive we are going to light signal fires around the entire building hopefully removing the escape route of the shadow men. The Gyants will be another matter. They are not scared of fire and they fight wickedly, arm your men with long spears if possible and bows."

Lord Aren nodded. "We will be there before midnight."

James nodded as he leaped back into the saddle. "We will look for you. Understand that this is probably our only chance to rescue your missing. If the shadow men have moved this quickly that means they are getting ready to flee and if they make good their escape all of the missing will be lost for good."

Lord Aren nodded, "We will arrive in time."

James pulled his mount around and followed by Cate and Keena he galloped through the medieval town of Graystone. They cleared the gatehouse even before the gates were fully open and pounded down the narrow dirt track as fast as their mounts could carry them.

It was about four miles back to the old Sauk Rapids Bridge and they covered it in less then an hour. When they arrived, James found Conner waiting impatiently on the far side of the log barrier, while nearly twenty nervous Graystone soldiers waited in a loose skirmish line where the concrete met the riverbank.

"Remove the barrier!" James cried as they skidded to a halt.

"On whose authority!"

"I don't have time for this," James growled. He motioned with his hand and the barrier gave an ominous creak, rose ponderously on its side, and then slipped over the edge into the river below with a tremendous splash.

"I wouldn't do that if I were you," Cate said suddenly in a deadly voice. Her shaft pointed at the young soldier who stepped forward and had leveled his bow at them. "Your Lord Aren is on his way and if he finds any of us harmed there will be hell to pay."

The soldier lowered his bow slowly as he gulped at the steely look in her eyes.

"Conner," James called as he waved the ruler of Quarry over to where they were. "Do you know the gray building that survived the Day the Sky Burned just south of here along the river?"

"Yes," Conner replied. "Some of the local farmers have reported that it is haunted. Many strange things have happened in that area lately, probably the work of Graystone spies keeping watch on our movements."

"Not now, Conner," James ordered sternly.

"I believe that is where the missing children are most likely being held." James explained. "We need to get there quickly and try to head off any escape while the men of Graystone move into position."

"You agreed to let them cross the river?" Conner said angrily.

"Would you rather fight this battle alone?" James asked. The question brought a silent glare from the Quarrian but he finally relented.

"Let's ride," Conner said. He motioned his men around and as one unit they charged off the bridge and broke into smaller groups as they passed through the forest that now separated the remains of down town St Cloud from the single remaining bridge.

26 A Queen

The Atwood Center was dark when they arrived, lit only by the moonbeams shining down from above. With the entrances darkened the building seemed ominous, almost like a creature of the night crouched and ready to pounce on any intruders.

"Quickly, light fires around the entire building," James ordered as he sent a dozen brilliant lights spinning around until every side was free of shadows. "And quickly, holding this number of lights is very draining."

Conner's men spread out gathering deadfall and limbs and stacking piles every twenty feet. Each time a pile was finished James sent a puff of flames into the tinder dry wood and smiled grimly as the ancient remains of trees sent flames rolling dozens of feet into the air. Within an hour the entire building was ringed in flames and Conner tasked half of his men with maintaining the circle of fire.

"Now, we will enter the lion's den," James said. He and Conner stood near the gaping entrance staring into the darkness. A stack of torches lay on the ground nearby and James reached down to light one of them. When the torch was burning brightly he stepped forward motioning Cate and

Conner to follow him. "Tell your men to bring as many torches as they can and keep their weapons handy."

The first twenty feet of the building showed that the structure had not escaped the meteor storm unharmed. Piles of rubble fallen into doorways blocked access to many of the rooms and even when James sent his light into the crevasses that still existed, nothing moved.

"James, you should see this," Keena called suddenly. Her voice barely above the hiss of the flames as she motioned down the last ten feet of hallway before another old cave in blocked their passage. "Something is down there."

James sent his light racing across the space surprising the hidden shadow man and bringing an unearthly wail from the creature.

Cate and Keena loosed their arrows immediately but the creature evaded the shafts and dropped into the ground. As they rushed forward it disappeared into a hidden shaft leading into the earth.

"Quickly, before it gets away." James rushed forward and leaped down into the wide hole in the ground. He dropped about eight feet and came to a soft landing in churned dirt. Nearby the shadow man slashed him with a clawed hand and missed. The nearly transparent creature turned and fled as Conner and two more soldiers scrambled into the ground and joined James. Cate and Keena followed moments after when a round of shouts echoed from down the long dark hall.

"What is happening?' James asked.

"Lord Aren has arrived but he brings word that Gyants have been spotted moving this way."

James looked up at the breathless soldier, "Tell him that he must find a way to fend the creatures off. We need time to search the tunnels."

2013: The End

The man nodded and then he was gone.

James turned back to the underground lair and the six of them advanced down into the ground. The tunnel around them was carved through dirt and rock and spanned nearly ten feet wide and an equal height. James could tell that the tunnel led them slowly into the ground but it seemed to drive in a straight path towards its goal.

All was quiet for several minutes as the fresh dirt on the ground deadened their steps but the silence was broken when several shadow men rushed forward slashing their clawed hands. One of Conner's men cried out and fell to the ground and pandemonium broke out in the confines of the tunnel. James took a step back as he brightened his globe of light; Cate loosed an arrow that passed so close to his head that he ducked involuntarily. Thankfully her aim remained perfect and one of the shadow men slumped to the ground with a shaft stuck almost completely through his head. Conner finally managed to stick a second with his sword and pinned it to the ground while his remaining soldiers struggled to land a blow that would finish the creature. There were at least two more shadow creatures but they fled seconds later leaving the small party with a mortally wounded member and leaving two of their own behind.

"Will he survive?" Keena asked. She wiped her dagger clean after helping Conner finally finish off the shadow man pinned under his sword.

"He has passed already," James replied as he checked for a pulse. The edges of the deep gashes had turned gangrenous already and his body lay on the ground stiffly. "Their claws are poisonous."

"Alright," Cate muttered. "Avoid the claws."

The tunnel finally opened up into what looked like a natural cavern and James spotted the big Queen Gyant immediately. Near her two of her soldiers stood watch over a huddled group of children that sat on the ground dejectedly. There was another rush towards them as they entered and James pushed his globe of light out until it hovered over them with the power of a million light bulbs. The shadow men cried out in pain and fell back trying to escape the sudden pain of the intense light.

There was a rush of movement and a chorus of cries as the children spotted them and came to the feet as one. The Queen and her two Gyants swept towards them with pincers grasping and seeking their blood. They seemed immune to the light and James watched as Keena and Cate released their shafts almost at the same time. He reached out with his mind and grabbed the bolts in mid flight using his power to create a dozen more and sending them racing at the two Gyants. One of the gyants tumbled to the ground and thrashed weakly about stuck through with eight arrows, but the other took the four shafts that struck it and continued its headlong charge.

"Come on then you stinking beast!" Conner cried. He ran forward with his sturdy spear held before him.

James cried out a warning but his strength was flagging and before he could act the Quarrian leader thrust hard with his spear and then disappeared under the gyant as it fell to the dirt. The Queen slowed as she approached and finally stopped less than a dozen feet away.

"God, she is an ugly thing," Keena muttered. Towering almost twenty feet in the air her faceted eyes stared down at them and her legs tapped nervously on the ground.

The Queen's swollen torso dragged heavily on the ground leaving streaks in the soft ground as she moved closer. A spasm wracked her body and behind her an egg slipped to the ground. Immediately a gyant's pincers pierced the egg sack and a smaller version of the two warriors broke free.

"Shoot it!" James called to Keena but she hesitated.

"It's just a baby," Keena growled as she sighted down her bow.

Cate loosed her own arrow and struck the smaller gyant in the torso bringing it to a halt, "It's a baby that will gut you in a heartbeat!" Cate notched another arrow and sent it at a higher angle but it struck the queen and shattered against her carapace. "James, do something." The queen used its legs to drag its body closer and the snapping of her pincers forced them to scatter.

James was weak already and he just barely managed to throw his body out of the way of the razor sharp pincers. He tried to bring down a wall of fire atop the queen but after a small burst of flame the fire dropped off and fizzled out of existence. Two more arrows struck the queen but only one of the managed to penetrate the carapace. James weakly pulled his body away from the queen who was now straddling the second of her dead warriors. Foot by foot he pushed his body back until he rested against the cool stones of the cavern wall. Again he called down fire atop her head and concentrated on holding the fire around her. The queen thrashed and screamed with an unearthly wail as her antennae wilted to the flames and her eyes were burned out permanently. Weakness filled James's body and he leaned back as the fire failed. Despite her horrible wounds the queen turned to where he lay and stumbled towards him, behind her three more of the eggs burst free from her and the warriors began breaking free despite the arrows directed at them from Cate and Keena.

As she approached, James leaned back, seeing his death in her scarred visage but then the impossible happened. The dead gyant warrior that had fallen on Conner suddenly heaved to the side and fell away; from the soft earth the Quarrian emerged covered in dirt but holding his spear in his hand. He glanced around the cavern taking in the situation and then he sprinted towards the queen and leaped onto her back. With amazing agility he raced across her back and slammed his spear deep into her spine.

A sudden surge of energy brought James back to his feet as he watched the gyant queen rear back and open her mouth with a wail of pain. Her legs skittered wildly and then she fell ponderously to the ground where the impact shook the entire cavern raining dirt and small pebbles down on them from the ceiling.

"Conner, thank god, I thought you had died," James cried with a tremendous smile. He stumbled to where the bloodied man was struggling to tear his spear from the remains of the gyant queen.

"Takes more than a gyant to stop me," Conner boasted. Suddenly his voice grew softer, "Honestly, this ugly creature nearly crushed me when she pulled her swollen body across that gyant that fell atop me." He leaned over and coughed violently spitting a wad of blood to the ground.

James used a bit of remaining power to scan Conner, he spotted the cracked ribs immediately but otherwise the warrior seemed fine, "Your ribs are broken but you should recover."

Both men turned and watched Cate and Keena put two arrows into the remaining smaller gyant. With all of the gyant now dead the group of children huddling in the corner rushed out to surround them smiling and cheering. Conner's nephew, Aden, grabbed his uncle in a bear hug and clung to him for dear life as great tears streamed down his cheeks.

When James felt he was strong enough to walk for a distance they gathered everyone together and began the trek back to the surface. It took all of them working together to lift the rescued children out of the pit. When they emerged from the Atwood Center James stopped and stared. The scene that greeted them was pulled from a nightmare. Nearly thirty gyants battled the combined forces of Lord Aren and Conner's men. The mounted Quarrians seemed to be faring well but still many horses with empty saddles were fleeing the battle. James watched as a group of ten Quarrians rushed a gyant that was separated from the safety of the battle line and pinned it to the ground with dozens of spear thrusts. Dozens of gyants were dead and scattered across the battered landscape. Lord Aren had drawn his army up in a tight formation and was smartly using his archers to pepper the gyants and draw them out to where his footmen could finish them off. The leader of Graystone faced a worse situation because his men were more heavily encumbered and unable to dodge the strikes from the gyant's pincers before killing the creatures.

Cate and Keena run towards the battle line immediately and put their more powerful bows to work. James tiredly began using what strength he had left to direct and add a bit of power to the arrows. Together the trio cut through the gyant ranks and destroying the cohesion of their formation. Once they began to scatter the Quarrians and men of Graystone finished the battle quickly.

"I am going to sleep soon," James said to Cate and Keena. "Don't let these kill each other and when I awake I will deal with making their alliance a bit more permanent."

Cate nodded, "We will keep watch over your body until you awaken."

Too exhausted to even nod his agreement James stumbled to a spot of grass that survived the battle and lay down on the ground. Carefully he gathered his cloak around him, set his staff inside the crook of his arm, closed his eyes, and drifted off to sleep.

27 His Will?

James awakened in his castle and still a bit tired but overall he felt well. He slipped out of bed and slipped his arms into his robe and left the ornate bedroom. Rose was waiting outside the castle near the small stand of trees where he had first met her.

"You were gone for a long time this time," Rose muttered with an injured tone. She kicked at the ground and rocked back and forth as though she was thoroughly irritated with him.

"I think my friend is causing trouble on earth," James explained. Together they sat down under the tree and watched the river flow by the buried rocks, white caps flashed about on the surface but never stayed for long. He told her of the kidnapped children and her face showed her anger at the actions.

"Why is he after children?" she asked.

"I don't know, but I felt his presence in the shadow men when I tried to see into his mind," James said. "Have there been times like this before?"

"Yes," Rose nodded. "There have been times when evil men have held sway but not for a long time. Always before there has been a great man, one who stepped forward to stop them. Merlin found his Arthur. Throughout time many of the men who chose the path of light have worked tirelessly behind the scenes to bring good men to power or at least limit the damage caused by evil men."

James nodded, "So, it is up to me to try and guide those that I can to better the world in any way I can."

"That is how many have done it in the past," Rose said. "But how you counter his presence is up to you. I can tell you that the presence of magical creatures like the gyants has not happened in thousands of years."

"How long?" James asked. "I mean since you have heard of anything like this happening?"

"I would say ten thousand years have passed," Rose replied after thinking for a time.

"Were you here then? Helping those who came?"

"Oh no," Rose laughed. "I am a mortal just like you, I will live and then when my time is past I will die. Even though I am a spirit, we still come and go in answer to His will."

"Whose?" James asked.

"That you must find out for yourself," Rose said with a smile. She turned and slipped back into her tree and was gone leaving James to ponder her cryptic answer.

When it was obvious to James that she was not coming back anytime soon, he returned to the castle behind him and lay back down in his bed. Tiredly he slipped off to sleep and as his body and mind rested his energy returned quickly. Three days later on earth he awoke.

The End - For Now

MATTHEW J KRENGEL

Matthew lives in the Sauk Rapids area of Minnesota with his family. He is an avid reader and writer and loves fantasy. After growing up in central Minnesota and attending college at Pensacola Christian College he moved back to Minnesota and began writing. His first book **Staff of Elements** was published in 2011 and he has a young adult fantasy **The Map Maker** being released by NorthStar Press this September. He is busy preparing several self published books and hopes someday to make writing his full time occupation. Visit his website at www.mjkbooks.com for regular updates.

Made in the USA
Charleston, SC
23 June 2012